MW00943941

A Woman and Her Dog

By Bonnie Jae Dane

Copyright © 2014 by Bonnie Jae Dane

Cover Art Nathan Evans

Good Tern Press

Boston, MA

1

Friends tell me I have a peculiar relationship with my dog, Lambert. They always begin their sentences with 'most people'. I know when I hear that opening phrase 'most people', a criticism will follow about my relationship with Lambert. Most people don't sleep with their dogs, most people don't take their dogs on dates with prospective husbands, and most people don't pay their hair stylist extra to groom the family pet after the salon's business hours. How do we really know what most people do? I want to tell my friends it's an arrogant assumption to express knowing what most people do and don't do. If I allowed my mind to dwell on what most people are doing behind their closed doors, it would probably turn my dreams into nightmares.

Lambert is the love of my life. The farmer I bought him from told me he was a Border Collie born too small to be effective at herding sheep. The farmer also said Lambert did not possess the true heart of a real Border Collie. I found his attitude condescending and at that moment when playing with Lambert at the vegetable stand along the side of the road, I knew Lambert was definitely smarter than his temporary owner when refusing to spend his days chasing sheep. Even when tied to the vegetable stand with a clothes line rope, Lambert knew being the love of someone's life was definitely better than being an overworked farm dog.

The farmer offered to give me Lambert for a hundred dollars, enough he said to cover the vet bills. Poor Lambert probably hadn't even seen a vet. I did try to talk my own doctor into giving him a physical exam, after hours of course, but he mumbled something about sanitation and fleas, and then had the nerve to give me a prescription for anti-anxiety medication. Lambert and I went immediately to Johns, my uptown hairstylist, who had a penchant for pretty boys and cross dressing. Half the time when I went to get my hair done, I didn't know whether Johns would be outfitted in haute couture or bib overalls sans shirt. Being privy to Johns' oddities, made it easier to approach him on the subject of Lambert's grooming needs. We settled on a regular Wednesday evening shampoo and blow dry appointment. Johns even referred us to his holistic vet friend, Maggie, who treated Charo, his tiny Chihuahua.

I really don't like the connotation of the word vet. Somehow the American Medical Association has managed to demean every other certified form of medical approach from vets to chiropractic, energy healers and even the Indian medicine man. I've often wondered how the AMA thinks we were all cured of our ailments long before they set themselves up as the final authority on medicine, while working from the town barber shop. That aside, Maggie combined energy healing with massage and occasional x-rays for broken bones when needed. She put her hands gently on Lambert's freshly coiffed hair and said he was in perfect health, a lovely dog, and a treasure to anyone's heart. Her words sang music to my ears when hearing my new companion described as a special being in my life.

I then visited an upscale dog boutique to search for a bed. I had never lived with a dog before and wasn't sure exactly where they preferred to sleep. I assumed they slept in beds similar to people beds only smaller. Mostly, I found large pillows and one canopy affair occupied by a small poodle much to its owner's dismay. She showed me the thousand dollar price tag, and I had to agree it cost more than my own bed plus the tiny mattress was extra along with a down comforter. I could tell Lambert sympathized with the fussy little dog when its mother scolded her for being spoiled. Later, I learned you cannot spoil a dog beyond its capacity to love. I glanced at Lambert with appreciation as we both decided on the Highland plaid pillow for large dogs. It possessed a masculine quality and accommodated Lambert's stocky body comfortably. The store clerk, a friendly woman of about sixty with long grey hair and a chic hippy look, agreed Lambert did appear comfortable, so much so he fell asleep on it while she showed me the rows of designer leashes and collars.

Clothes shopping for myself always seemed to be a formidable task. Even sending me into fits of hysteria if the image in the dressing room mirror didn't match the image I had in my mind. Usually, I left the store without buying a thing and thus my clothes closet remained empty of pretty dresses but instead contained simple flax ensembles of dusky colors, which fortunately matched my short bobbed auburn hair with blonde highlights. At least it appeared as though I had put some thought into my personal care. Now, I found myself responsible for choosing the right accessories for my new black and white dog. I glanced at the clerk Karma, that's what her name tag read, in bewilderment. Karma seemed to understand immediately and asked, "Is Lambert your first dog?"

"Yes. Is it obvious?" I asked and sighed even more over the responsibility of now having a dependent. I didn't even know if I was supposed to declare Lambert on my income tax form.

"Oh, honey, it became obvious to everyone in the store when we saw you enter carrying your Border Collie, a breed known for being intelligent enough to walk."

"I don't have a leash for him, yet, and I was worried we might be arrested because of the leash laws." I tried to defend myself.

"Yes, it's a shame about leash laws. The geese should have to wear a leash. They're more problematic than dogs. Besides that, a Border Collie doesn't really need a leash, honey; he'll not leave your side on account of being a herding dog." She smiled prettily. I hadn't thought about his herding instinct. Maybe the farmer was wrong, and when giving it some thought, Lambert seemed disinclined to be out of my line of vision. I tossed a loving glance in the direction of his sleeping form and noticed one eye was opened and watching me. He then stood, ambled over and inspected the rows of collars with matching leashes, as though puzzling over which one to choose. My affection for him swelled, and then he did the most amazing thing. He stood on his hind legs and grabbed the red plaid collar matching his pillow. Even Karma looked surprised over his decisiveness.

"Border Collies want to please their person. He sensed your confusion," Karma said. We both studied Lambert's happy face and smiled.

"I wonder if he could help me with my own clothes shopping." My seriousness made the sales clerk laugh. She carried Lambert's accoutrements to the counter, and asked me if I wanted some dog treats from their bakery. Lambert already had his nose pressed against the glass case.

I discovered I could not deny Lambert anything. We went home with his bed, matching blanket, matching collar and leash, toothpaste, toothbrush, cot, traveling water bottle, assorted chew toys and a stuffed kitty Lambert picked out for himself, not to mention a baker's dozen of homemade dog cookies covered with carob icing.

The first night after we brought home Lambert's new bedding, he piled his body on top of it for about thirty minutes before I could feel his paw patting my shoulder. I rolled over to see his brown eyes backlit from the moon shining in my bedroom window. His eyes stared pleadingly into mine, and I wondered if he was unhappy and exactly what he wanted at midnight that wasn't already provided for him. I petted his head and closed my eyes, but again I felt an urgent pressing of his paw on my arm. "What is it, boy?" I asked. Lambert tended to respond to questions and life in general through actions rather than a wordy dialogue about his needs. One leap and he was settled in next to me with his head on the pillow. I noticed he had made some effort to pull his own blanket over his shoulders. We both slept until the alarm rang at 7:00 am.

Lambert tossed his new leash on my slippers before I had a chance to dress and think about breakfast. I suddenly realized I would be going for an unaccustomed early morning walk, no doubt, for the next sixteen years of my life. I tended to be on the lazy side, only exercising my brain while my almost forty year old body remained inert and slightly amorphous and well-hidden under my expensive but shapeless flax ensembles.

I threw on some clothes and followed Lambert to the front door. We stepped outside and smelled the cool morning air for about two seconds before Lambert pulled me off the front steps to jog down the sidewalk. Another few seconds and I was winded with a stitch in my side, but Lambert kept moving at a brisk pace, occasionally stopping to water someone's bushes and then hurry on as though he had some place important to go. By the time we returned to our front door, my tongue hung to the ground and sweat filled my eyes and trickled into my mouth. Not a pretty sight. Fortunately, no one appeared, or at least so I thought until hearing a raspy, disapproving voice call my name.

"Heddy!"

Yes, my name is Heddy Lowe, successful artist, single, living in a cozy bungalow, and a failure at love. My front door rarely opened to welcome an eager date; mostly men who were sent by a well-intentioned friend rang my door bell and always seemed more interested in my art work than me. So my having a dog would spark some neighborhood interest.

"Yes, Mr. Dodder!" I wiped the sweat from my eyes with a loose sleeve. Lambert seemed annoyed by the interruption and sniffed our neighbor like he was a foul odor gone sour from being left out in the sun too long.

"What you got here is a Border Collie." He stated this obvious fact like it was an accusation. Lambert, considerably offended, lifted his leg and managed to pee a couple of drops on Mr. Dodder's work shoes. "See here. You have no business keeping a Border Collie. They're working dogs. He'll run you ragged. Best take him back." He said this with finality while wiping the wet spot off his shoe by rubbing it on the back of the other pant leg.

"Mr. Dodder, I appreciate your concern but no need to worry. I have lots of work to keep him busy." I made this up, of course. I really had no clue why this came out of my mouth and exactly what job to give Lambert that would make him feel useful.

"Mark my words, little lady." He called over his shoulder as he stepped into an old truck, which I considered an eyesore. Lambert sensing my aggravation lifted his leg on the truck's well-worn tire and then walked up our front steps and waited for me to open the door.

I filled his bowl with kibble and sat down to ponder exactly what would add meaning to Lambert's life. I often went to the country side and scouted for picturesque landscapes worthy of putting on canvas. Perhaps, Lambert would like to go along with me and run in the fields while I worked at my easel. Karma had added a harness to his accessories so he could be buckled safely in the passenger seat; she also mentioned the need to travel with his water bottle and some treats. An hour and a half later we both drove along the New England country roads and let our eyes roam the stone fences and rolling hills. I usually turn landscapes into abstracts, giving them a lilting Japanese quality not often seen in art galleries. I supposed this helped to distinguish them among the other more literal interpretations. The galleries put significant price tags on them and gave me sixty percent of the sales. I never thought much about money. It always appeared in my bank account thanks to a good money manager. I wondered what he would think when I asked him to set up a trust fund for Lambert.

Suddenly, Lambert barked for me to stop. He began wagging his tail and pointing his wet nose in the direction of the loveliest red barn I had seen in a long time. A tractor with a well-worn patina had been parked next to it. Both the barn and tractor possessed a slightly ramshackle appearance perfect for my canvas. I hugged Lambert who gave me a hearty lick up the side of my face and seemed quite pleased with accomplishing his first job.

I hauled all my equipment to the barn packed neatly on a small dolly, including a portable dog cot for Lambert along with his traveling water bottle and snacks. Lambert carried my canvas bag of paints in his mouth and trotted directly to the barn. Actually, I decided to get a feel for the tractor. The patina combined mostly greys, blues and some rust once covered in black primer. Perfect. I set up and began painting. Lambert helped arrange his cot and bowls, got himself a snack and went off to explore his surroundings. The next several hours flew by.

When finished I noticed Lambert laid sleeping on his cot with straw and wildflower petals stuck all over his coat. His water bowel had been emptied and the snacks demolished along with the bag Karma had packed them in. He's definitely a boy I thought while gazing lovingly at my new companion. I reached over and patted his head to wake him up. He yawned, stood, and shook himself and then grabbed my canvas bag of paints and headed back to our station wagon.

Once home, we both jumped from the car and began unpacking. Again a raspy voice interrupted our good time.

"Been out in the fields, Heddy. Yuh dog's covered in dead weeds." Mr. Dodder stuck his head over the back fence.

"Lambert will take a bath." I didn't exactly know what I was talking about here. I'd never bathed a dog and hoped Johns might be able to give him a quick shampoo.

"Betta check fuh ticks! All I got to say!"

"Thanks, Mr. Dodder. Will do." Lambert and I hurried in the back door with our supplies and dropped everything on the kitchen floor. He slurped the water out of his bowl while I checked my phone for messages.

"Hi, I'm Tim Randall. Karma at the King Charles Boutique told me you were in with your new dog. Said we might have a lot in common because of my new spaniel Buffy. Would you like to meet for coffee tonight? It's Bark 'n Beer night at the West End Café. 8:00 pm. Looking forward."

"He didn't leave a number, Lambert. And what's Bark 'n Beer. Oh, well, would be fun to get out for a while. What do you think, boy?" Lambert barked happily and smiled, then turned and opened the cupboard door where I kept the kibble. He dragged the bag next to his bowl. I had no idea dogs were so smart. "Okay, then. I'll take a shower and call Johns and ask if he can fit you in." More barks while I filled his bowl.

Johns unlocked the salon door and motioned for us to go to the back room where the staff gathered during breaks.

"Oh, Doll, what a day. Eight grey heads with no imagination. I tell them a whimsical cut would look darling if they want to stay grey or why not a few streaks of magenta. Oh my Gawd, Heddy, the caterwauling could be heard in Idaho. What's a girl to do?" Johns sashayed to the back room wearing his trade mark bibs with no shirt.

"You could let your own hair go grey and that of at least two of your over age fifty hair stylists. Show your older clientele how chic they can look," I suggested.

"Oh, Honey, why so bitchy?"

"Johns, I've known you for twenty years and have no idea what your real hair color is. Besides, you'd look great with a few strands of grey all punked and sassy."

"You think, doll?"

"Sure do."

"I'll consider it. Now let's take care of my last client. Come on Lambert jump in the bowl." Lambert dragged the step stool to the counter, climbed each step and then leaped into the bowl, sitting perfectly still.

"My Charo doesn't respond to commands. I have to do everything for her. Lambert is more cooperative than most of my clients." Johns sighed and gently lathered shampoo bubbles all over my happy dog.

Lambert and I sat at an outside table and ordered an iced tea for me and a bowl of water for him.

"We have to charge $3.00 for water, miss, no matter who's drinking it."

"That's okay. And bring some corn chips and salsa."

"For you or your dog?"

"Does it matter since it cost the same?"

"Coming right up."

I looked around for someone Karma would think highly enough of to talk about Lambert and my visit to her store, and then it occurred to me, Karma knew nothing about me except my incompetence as a new dog owner. The other diners glanced in our direction, smiled and turned back to their beers. I don't have any outstanding features to attract stares, so they were probably admiring Lambert sitting upright in his chair sniffing at the odors wafting from the kitchen. Finally, the waitress brought our order and carefully arranged everything in place before tearing off the bill and handing it to Lambert. I laughed and again people glanced over at us and smiled. Just then, a tall man appeared and said you must be Heddy, and this is Lambert. He introduced himself as Tim Randall and pulled up a chair. He was a handsome man, self-assured and slightly too good to be true for a blind date. I listened intently to his small talk, so I could catch sight of all the red flags.

"Has Lambert been to obedience school?"

"No. Why? Does he appear to need his manners refined?"

"Well, usually dogs don't sit at the table in a restaurant."

I glanced around at all the flannel shirted men hunkered over their beers, gnawing on ribs and corn cobs.

"Not exactly fine dining, Tim. Besides, where is he supposed to sit?" I asked testily. Lambert picked up my tone and brought his paw down on Tim's hand and leaned into it. I could tell Tim felt the unfriendly pressure of an offended canine.

"Stronger than he looks." He retrieved his hand and rubbed the red out of it.

"Quite."

"Sorry, we've got off to a bad start. I'm a dog trainer and Karma thought you could use some assistance in managing your new companion."

"You mean you're here trolling for new business?" My voice rose and a red flush went up my neck and darkened my face. I felt the heat of anger, not a normal emotion for a person who keeps to herself.

"Well, that sounds mercenary when you put it that way. No, I am single and looking to settle down with a dog lover. I think Karma thought I could combine the two. Actually, I'm not sure what she had in mind. I'm sorry if I offended you."

"You didn't offend me. You offended Lambert. I'm the one who needs training on caring for him." I reached over and wiped the corn chips off Lambert's mouth with his napkin and laid it on the table. He took a further swipe on the napkin just in case I missed a few crumbs.

"Yes, I see. He is extraordinary." We both stared at Lambert. Just then he dipped the last corn chip in the salsa bowl and ate it. I wondered how a farm dog could have inherent good manners.

I put a twenty on the table next to the bill and stood to leave. Lambert jumped down and followed me to the station wagon. I could hear Tim's voice call after me. "Couldn't we start over?"

I kept going. Once home, I threw myself on the couch and cried till my eyes hurt. Lambert licked the tears from my face and pressed his nose against my neck to comfort me. No man would ever be so sweet and gentle. They would tell you to suck it up and take a warm bath. At least that had been my experience. I couldn't believe I had showered and even put on some lipstick for a man I thought was a date, only to discover he was courting me for business.

I began pouring out my dating woes to Lambert. Even told him about the time I caulked the bath tub and put in a new shower head just in case my previous disaster wanted to spend the night snoring happily in my bed, but no, he left shortly after I gave him what he really wanted, a list of contacts in the New York art scene. When I asked him why he felt the urgency to end our date at 9:00 pm, he said I wasn't his type because I was too sweet. I became uncharacteristically angry and began screaming at him, calling him low life names, which apparently turned him on because the next thing I knew my disinterested date was pawing my flax. I shoved him out the door and the last noise I heard was his excited voice yelling 'I love a woman with a fiery temper'. I continued to talk to Lambert for an hour, listing all my humiliations while trying to find a nice man for myself. He shook his head sympathetically and nuzzled my hair. I began to laugh. Yes, Lambert definitely up until that very moment was the sweetest male to grace my sorry love life.

Early the next morning the phone rang. Karma's voice sounded distressed and apologetic. She said she had told Tim about me. He recognized my name she said and asked what I thought about his calling me. Said she didn't think I would mind hearing from such a handsome man, but thought he really wanted a date and wasn't looking for business.

"I'm so sorry. He told me you got up and left him there feeling stupid. Said he misjudged the situation. I'm sorry, Heddy. I really thought you two would enjoy each other's company. I hope we can be friends. I'll put aside a baker's dozen for Lambert. It'll be my treat for making such a mess."

"I'll be all right. Don't worry. Just please don't give out my number to anyone else. I'll pick up Lambert's treat on our way to work."

"Oh, okay," she said. I could tell she wondered what roll Lambert played in my work. I hung up and got dressed for our early morning walk.

We walked into town and banged on Karma's door. Why make Lambert wait until we were headed to the countryside, I thought. The sign said closed, so I figured she might still be preparing for the day or in her back room bakery, putting together Lambert's snacks. She opened the door smiling as though happy to see us, and why not, at the very least we would be good customers. Lambert spotted a plaid bandanna matching his pillow and collar. He yanked it from the rack and tossed it on the counter. "Maybe I should open an account here," I said and pulled a credit card from my fanny pack.

Karma laughed and patted Lambert's head in appreciation for all of his business. She tied the bandanna around his neck and then complimented him on his handsome good looks. He jerked his head up and trotted back and forth in front of us like he was a run way model. Karma laughed again, and even I smiled with a mother's pride, although at this point, I had no idea what my role was in Lambert's life. We left with his bag of treats and hurried home to start another busy day.

The painting of the scenic tractor needed a lot more work, so I gathered up our gear and packed the station wagon. This time I prepared a bag lunch for myself and filled a thermos with iced tea.

"Yuh gonna make a sissy outta yuh dog what with that fancy hanky tied round his neck. Not right. Waste of a good working dog." Mr. Dodder watched us pack the car with a perplexed mixture of curiosity and disapproval.

"It's all right, Mr. Dodder. Lambert keeps plenty busy helping me."

"Yuh don't look like yuh need any help," he said and began to walk away.

This last remark caught me off guard, caused me to become indignant and even aggravated my patience for the unsolicited comments from an old man who, himself, needed to get a job.

"Mr. Dodder, if you spent your time doing something useful like crafting table chairs in your makeshift tool shop garage, you might not be so distressed over whether or not my dog is being put to good use."

"Yup, maybe gotta point. Still makin a sissy outta a good dog," Mr. Dodder yelled out his truck window as he drove slowly down our joint driveway. Lambert sensed my change of mood and barked after him.

I chattered to Lambert along the way, mostly about people being our greatest annoyance and my efforts to understand why. He seemed to agree and would occasionally glance over at me and nod sympathetically. Maybe that was why I didn't bother painting them but instead preferred to render the beauty of an inanimate object and the loveliness of nature. Even an old boat decaying in the harbor held more beauty to me than the underpinnings of a person's heart. I rolled my mind over the insistence people have in helping others improve their lives while their own remains in shambles too frightening to improve with considerable introspection and a serious rehab job. Yes, I thought the inner workings of people's minds must be too complex to bear scrutiny, and that's why it was easier for them to offer advice to their neighbors. Of course, this last thought prompted lengthy speculation on why Mr. Dodder felt the need to comment on Lambert's comings and goings. I wondered if Mr. Dodder did indeed feel useless and projected his feelings of being underutilized onto Lambert. If so, he should be more of an object of compassion rather than my disgruntlement.

Lambert and I agreed to take a different view of the old man living next door. Maybe ask him to make a frame for one of my paintings. I really didn't care for the amateurish quality of my own temporary frames and the possibility of shipping them to the galleries with more refined edges appealed to me. Yes, I said to Lambert, in conclusion, that's what we'll do. Sometime in the not too distant future, I added, giving myself time to calm down some from Mr. Dodder's last remark about my looking like I didn't need any help. This I construed referred to my not appearing like some fragile female in need of brute strength from the nearest man. "Besides Lambert," I said, "If I need a man to help me lift something, I'll hire one. Right boy?" He barked and we rolled into our parking spot and began to unpack.

I always lose myself while painting, which I view as a good thing. Quite frankly I, too, feel no need to peek inside my own mind to find out what is really going on there that keeps me from having a man devoted to my true essence. Actually, I don't even know what I'm talking about here, because I have no idea what the word essence really means when it pertains to the distillation of what makes up the real me. I read women's magazine but find them inane and counter to everything that happened in our mothers' generation. I mean did the women then fight for our rights as individuals only to have us reading the latest diet craze or which eye shadow gives our eyes the most depth? I mean, we should be looking at our own depth. But, as mentioned, I too am a coward when it comes to scrutinizing my inner self. I much prefer to slap my paint brush on a canvas and see what comes from the hither regions of my mind, eluding all self-scrutiny. And if I did possess an honest understanding of what comprises my entire being, my inner self, true self, essence, or the workings of an undisturbed mind, would I still feel the need to find clarity on canvas? Most probably I would wallow in the smugness of knowing I possess inherent value and not feel a need to do anything. At least my ignorance keeps me busy.

Again several hours passed with my paint brush joyfully speculating which colors reflect the patina of an old tractor. My paint brush worried over the light reflecting from the early afternoon sun. The light had become more intense than the previous day. This required me to contemplate an entirely different perspective of my bulky subject. Just when caught up in this dilemma, I glanced over the field to see Lambert tugging on a man's arm. The man looked like Lady Chatterley's lover in D.H. Lawrence's novel, only slightly out of context. I wondered why they were headed in this direction, but before I could formulate a plausible answer, Lambert pulled the larger than life character right in front of my canvas and then sat down as though satisfied with a job well done. Needless to say, I had no idea what Lambert considered his job to be. The poor man stammered in an effort to explain his presence.

"Is this your dog?" he said. He had a nicely clipped beard, wore a black T-shirt neatly tucked in his blue jeans held up by a belt buckle reading Harley Davidson. I dismissed him immediately as a man's man, no doubt, relegating women to the position of kitchen maid, always stirring a pot of soup on the stove. All this ran through my mind in under three seconds.

"Yes, his name is Lambert. Is there some reason why Lambert brought you here?"

"I have no idea. I was working in the back woods clearing some underbrush when he grabbed me by the arm and began pulling me in this direction. Seemed determined, so I figured someone was in trouble." He patted Lambert's head.

"Oh, I'm so sorry. You own this land, and I'm trespassing. I'll get packed in no time."

"No, you don't have to leave. Stay and paint anything you want. Just concerned about your dog."

"Well, Lambert has a personal agenda. I'm sure he just likes you and wanted us to meet." I realized immediately Lambert considered me incompetent to handle my own love life and decided to prowl around for a suitable mate.

"Well, he's one smart dog, then. I'm Daniel Loggins." He held out his hand for me to shake. He had a nice warm grip, didn't crush any of my bones, and didn't let his hand lay limp in mine. I liked his open face and toothy smile. Not magazine handsome but more lumberjack.

"Heddy Lowe." I shook his hand and smiled my best smile. I glanced at Lambert who appeared to be quite proud of himself. I had no idea what to do with the man Lambert had rustled up for me.

"I was about to take a break for lunch back at the house. Would you and Lambert care to join me?" Lambert wagged his tail and drooled.

"That's very nice, but I think we had better be going." I began packing my gear and indicated for Lambert to pull himself together and pick up my paints. I could feel my face turn red from embarrassment.

"Well, it was an unexpected pleasure to meet you and Lambert. I hope you come back tomorrow. I'll make sure to have lunch ready. I make a mean vegetarian chili." He grinned, causing me to lose a grip on my mind and begin running toward the car pulling my dolly behind me. A disgruntled Lambert plodded along beside me carrying my bag of paints.

I spent the evening staring at the tractor painting. It needed more work but not something that couldn't be done in my studio. I had no real reason to go back to Daniel Loggins' farm, unless I wanted to paint the barn, or unless I wanted a bowl of vegetarian chili. I then began to wonder if I had misjudged Lambert's choice of men. He probably wasn't a serial killer. Lambert wouldn't have dragged him across the field and deposited him at my feet if he thought the man was dangerous. It occurred to me Lambert had an uncanny knack for sniffing out people who would be an asset to his life and now to mine. My own faulty judge of character had always ended in disaster. Why not trust my dog to choose the people who would occupy space in our lives without creating chaos. Now that I gave the matter some thought, Lambert had peed on Mr. Dodder, slobbered over Johns, subtly assaulted Tim Randall, and tolerated Karma, all appropriate reactions to their behaviors. I could learn something from him.

I decided it might also help to study the profile of a vegetarian. A few clicks on the computer and up pops twenty studies done on the character traits of vegetarians. Most chose not to eat meat because they could not tolerate the suffering of animals. Some for spiritual reasons, a few for health reasons and one little boy spoke eloquently on not having a dead animal in his stomach. His mother, out of respect, prepared brown rice and vegetables for him. Also, surprisingly according to an article in the British Medical Journal vegetarians have higher IQs when children than their peers. The little boy pacifist seemed to exemplify this last finding.

During my silent ponderings, Lambert sulked on his new pillow, occasionally glancing in my direction to make sure I noticed he was not happy with me.

"Okay, Lambert, tomorrow we will go back to the farm and finish painting. If you're new friend invites us to lunch, we'll stay. Okay, boy?"

Lambert leaped from his pillow to the couch and licked my face with such glee, that I knew without a doubt my new companion had successfully put himself in charge of my life and well, maybe it would be in my best interest.

2

Lambert Weighs In:

Underneath all my fur lived an extended family of fleas along with several ticks and probably a few bed bugs. Sometimes, I enjoyed chasing sheep, but I always minded supporting the uninvited guests who used my body as a housing development. The itching alone sent me into a flurry of scratching that left welts on my tender skin. Farm life may appear idyllic in the eyes of people who live in city apartments, and even the dogs who reside there imagine themselves running free in the fields with wings on their feet and all the nonsense that make up their fantasy dreams. Nope, farm life tired my hairy butt and put a crimp in my natural inclination for a more refined lifestyle.

The day that idiot farmer tied me to a clothes line rope and shoved me into the back of his truck without respect to my dignity, turned into the day that would change my down-home life into a suburban paradise. I sniffed all the customers pawing through his vegetables until I finally got a whiff of sweetness. It came from a lady who spent at least fifteen minutes examining the apple baskets placed on the table where my rope was tied to the leg. It allowed me to take my time analyzing the smells emanating from her well-scrubbed body. The acrylic paint odors meant she must be an artist thus the reason for excessive showers using hypoallergenic soap. It also meant she would be able to take me to work; no lingering smells of a man; must be lonely and in need of a companion; naturally I slipped myself into that role if I played my cards right; slight traces of meat, a grocery store carnivore; loves butterscotch, leftover candy wrappers were in her pocket; and no sweat smells meant she remained calm in most situations and possessed an even temperament but not stupid. This last observation was gleaned from her conversation with the idiot farmer.

"Most of these apples are bruised," the apple lady said.

"Eat around the bruises." Idiot Farmer.

"Must be last year's apples. They're probably mealy." Apple Lady

"Naw, Missy, picked them this morning." Idiot Farmer.

"But, it's June. Apples are a fall fruit." Apple Lady sighed and put the one in her hand back in the basket. I leaned gently against her pant leg and sighed with her.

Apple Lady bent down and looked into my sympathetic eyes. I then quickly changed expressions to soulful, which is how I've heard people describe their dew- eyed fluff ball dogs, and then the owners themselves go all dewy eyed and a long conversation ensues on the antics of their canine MENSA candidates. I realized I wasn't exactly dignifying my superior breed by trying to rise above my working class background, but let those living without fleas cast a disapproving glance on my upwardly mobile aspirations. They can kiss my hairy butt.

"Oh, what a darling dog." Apple Lady spoke to no one in particular. This again reassured me she had lived alone too long and was in need of a companion. I placed my chin gently on her shoulder and sighed happily. I even nuzzled her neck and gave a tiny lick to the side of her face, promising even more affection if only I were hers. She bought it. The next thing I knew, Apple Lady tossed some money at the idiot farmer and put me in the passenger side of her car.

I waved goodbye to country life. No more sleeping outdoors with the sheep or having to worry excessively over losing one of their whiney babies who didn't have enough sense to stay close to its own mother. I felt like breaking out into an excited bark but knew it was important to appear to be the model dog during my probationary period or at least until Apple Lady became so attached to me she thought my gaseous toots were charming.

My new home smelled of disinfectant and lemons. It smelled clean and when first entering, I dragged my hairy butt across the carpet just to feel something soft beneath my tired body. I spun around like this for a full minute before noticing the perplexed expression on my new roommate's face. I stopped immediately and began a high stepping prance uncharacteristic to my breed but nevertheless impressive to those who didn't know any different. She began to laugh. I liked the sound of her laughter. It sounded like music. The idiot farmer never laughed and, in fact, his facial muscles had been permanently fixed into a disgruntled frown. No fun there. I kept this routine up until I noticed her sniff the air and then when she brought her nose closer, I knew the foul smell was coming from me. I thought for sure I would be given my walking papers when she hurried me back into her car.

Apple Lady parked the car on the side of a busy street. The noise hurt my ears, which hitherto this experience had never heard anything louder than an annoying woodpecker or the nightly vigil of a barn owl. Honking cars and thunderous voices assaulted my ears just before we entered a series of rooms smelling of chemicals similar to the ones used to dip a parasitic infested sheep.

A girly man greeted us with such enthusiasm I wondered what species he belonged to. Men with high-pitched giggling voices didn't live on the farm, so I had never met one. He also wore a dress, which was uncharacteristic of farmers who generally bought their pants from the Feed & Grain store. He seemed harmless enough and even gave me a cookie from a big jar, as though I were a three year old tot, accessorizing its mother. I didn't mind being patronized and ate the cookie in one swallow and hoped for more. Apple Lady called the girly man Johns. She and Johns laughed a lot together, which made me happy and calmed my fears about returning to the farm. Actually, the moment Johns set my body in a large bowl and sprayed it with water, I knew I was being domesticated to fit easily into my new roommate's social life. I didn't know Johns seemed to be the extent of her human companionship. I would have a lot to make up for.

We then experienced some kind of contretemps with her personal doctor who thought dogs belonged on the farm, and even though I smelled like a perfumed hooker, the man still treated me like a back alley cur, which in itself would have been a step up from my humble beginnings. Finally, after a quick phone call to Johns and a few tears from Roommate, we found our way to an animal doctor named Maggie. She seemed happy to meet me and even offered me a chair, where I placed my hairy butt. It put me nose to nose with a fussy little fur ball named Jack. His face looked like it had been hit with the underside of a shovel. It was that flat. I wondered how he breathed. I even worried about having to resuscitate the little guy should he be unable to get enough air through his tiny flat nose. He smelled like a dog. No fleas or ticks on this guy, but still, he had an expression of sadness that could have made my heart cry had I not seen his person kiss the top of his head and tell Apple Lady about Jack's ability to use the cat door. I nearly shit bricks when learning how little humans actually expected of us. It made me ponder my own importance in the world and for a moment I lapsed into philosophical thought on the meaning of existentialism in the canine world. However, my lofty ponderings were interrupted by a real mean son of a bitch dog calling himself Rottweiler Ralph, a nuisance breed to our species so far as I was concerned.

Instinct took over when the vicious RR regarded Jack's pampered butt with disgust. He snarled with such menace, Jack embarrassed our species by trying to hide in his owner's purse. I stood on my chair, which I must admit made me appear taller, and growled with similar intensity. RR quieted down and remained across the room. I must admit I had absolutely nothing in my arsenal of weapons to fend off an attack should he decide to drag Jack's pathetic butt from his mom's purse, but I continued with the occasional snarl and was grateful my human companion didn't put my life at risk by treating me like a girly dog.

Finally, Dr. Maggie called us to the examination room. Flute music played on the small stereo and tiny bottles of medicines and oils filled shelves lining one entire wall. I had never been in a room intended to calm the patient's frazzled nerves. Even a small water fountain had been plugged into the wall and circulated water intensifying the rain forest feel. I expected a cockatoo to fly across the room. I watched

Roommate glance around at our surroundings. She appeared pleased at the ambiance and settled into the subtle calculation of a doctor who had enough good sense to calm the patient before telling him he had testicular cancer or some other frightening disease.

I still had my balls intact, but heard the Doctor talking to Roommate about the benefits of neutering a male dog. I could feel both my balls shrivel inside their animal bag and disappear altogether. Dr. Maggie talked so casually about this procedure, only taking a few minutes and yes, the patient would be put under and might be sleepy for a few hours. If done in the early morning, she went on, Roommate could pick up the patient by 5:00 pm. My ears strained to hear the outcome of this conversation.

"I don't know. Seems like mutilation." Roommate.

"No. They feel nothing. And they don't really need them. It makes males more docile and keeps the dog population under control." Dr. Maggie the Butcher.

"Still though, I have to consider Lambert's point of view. I'll talk to one of my male friends." Roommate.

"Yes, well, other than neutering, Lambert's in perfect health. I'll give you something natural to prevent fleas and ticks." Dr. Maggie.

We sat in the car for a few minutes while Roommate stroked the back of my neck and patted my head. I could get use to someone actually touching me with affection. Prior to this experience, my body had only been touched by the idiot farmer's boot. Even the sheep never made physical contact but seemed to regard me with halfhearted indifference, which in the idiot farmer's eyes did make me appear useless as a herding dog. I could hear myself sigh. Roommate studied her phone and then finally decided to make a call to Johns. She related the conversation with Dr. Maggie regarding the future of my balls. The shriek coming from the phone caused my ears to hurt. Somehow the conversation went from being about my genitals to covering Johns' hysterical attachment to his own. Roommate spent another few minutes calming her friend while continuing to stroke my furry body. I lay down in the passenger seat and enjoyed the massage but still kept an ear cocked to hear the upshot of their conversation.

"You're right. I wouldn't want Lambert's male dignity to be snipped. And yes, I agree. I couldn't possibly understand what it would be like to have mine removed. Thanks Johns."

I gathered from their conversation my balls had been given a reprieve. I wagged my tail and Roommate upon seeing this display of happiness pressed her face against my fur and told me how much she loved me. I hadn't expected to be taken so completely into the embrace of a human person nor anyone for that matter. I nearly cried but immediately got ahold of my dignity and instead licked the side of her face, which made her giggle. I would have to stop calling her roommate or apple lady. The sudden evolving of our relationship would require me to search my mind for an intimate term of endearment. I had heard Jack call the woman holding his pampered butt, Mom, and so I decided Mom seemed to be an appropriate title for the one who would be filling my food bowl for the rest of my life. My biological mom had hardly made an impression on me once Idiot Farmer had dumped me and my siblings into a bucket of warm cow's milk and sent her back to work. Life took funny turns if you let go of all the notions of how you think things should be.

I felt like I had put in a full day by the time we returned to my new house. Did I mention the small back yard had a wooden fence slightly too high for me to jump over should I feel like roaming the neighborhood? However, I noticed the gate had a simple latch that only required me to push it up and sideways to open if I get restless and feel the need to take a stroll around the block. Closing the gate and securing the latch would require a complicated maneuver but easily done with a few practice tries whenever Mom wasn't looking. I had to bite myself for this lapse into my natural inclination to be a cagey cur, a personality trait adopted from being the runt of the litter, no doubt. My lowly position had required constant maneuvering just to get enough milk to sustain myself.

I took in the small expanse of yard. I had never seen grass without weeds and those yellow dandelion flowers that seemed to be an annoyance to most homeowners. The idiot farmer dragged his big sloppy feet across his yard creating dirt paths everywhere. He didn't mind the yellow flowers and assorted weeds that grew freely around the dirt patches. I put that thought behind me and unabashedly threw my body on the perfectly trimmed two inch grass and rolled the perfume off my fur with the hopes of replacing it with the fecund smell of topsoil.

The raspy sound of an old codger interrupted my suburban bucolic communion.

"I see yuh got yuhself a dog, Heddy." Old Codger.

"Yes, Mr. Dodder. This is Lambert." Mom glowed with pride.

"Lambert's a good name. Strong. Let's hope he lives up to it." Old Codger.

"He already has." Immediately an image of Rottweiler Ralph entered Mom's awareness. I picked up the image and knew she thought of me as a brave dog for taking on the waiting room bully. I could feel myself puff up from my own pride. I stood and pranced toward the back door.

"Walking like a Lipizzan stallion. Got airs. May have to knock them outta him befuh he gets too full himself. Farm dog, Heddy. " said the Old Codger.

Obviously, the old codger had problems keeping his nose on his side of the fence. I had heard Idiot Farmer's wife talking about all their farm neighbors. She verbally shredded them for being lazy good-for-nothings when they didn't get their hay bailed before the first frost. She then went on to roast the villagers with the Butane torch she called a tongue. By the time she finished searing all the human persons, she caught sight of my hairy butt and told her idiot husband she had no intention of feeding something that looked like the cat dragged home. That's when he got the notion to take me to the vegetable stand. I still smarted from the memory of being referred to as something the cat dragged home. I knew you couldn't get any lower than that. Fortunately, Mom saw nothing but good in me. She patted my head after closing the door on Old Codger's last words.

"Shud be sleeping outside, Missy."

The old codger had the potential to become the bane of my new existence. I idled on this thought for a while, leaning my head against Mom's leg sighing with the sounds of resignation. Mom patted me again. I wagged my tail and let the unpleasant thoughts roll off me. Life couldn't get any better.

The next day we went to a store filled with dog accessories and a bakery specializing in canine treats. I nearly peed myself from excitement, but realized I now trotted alongside the lives of civilized beings who definitely had a different view of all their natural biological functions. I mused over Mom having a separate room used to relieve her bladder. She could just as easily pee around the perimeters of her own yard. Human persons would continue to baffle me. I wondered for a moment if I was supposed to hike a leg over the porcelain chair, but it didn't seem to be the case, because she had opened the back door every two hours and told me to go tinkle. Again, I stress people's need to give euphemisms to all their bodily functions. Took me the longest time to figure out what the sound 'poo' meant. Then I realized she couldn't bring herself to make references to all the turds I had left lying around the backyard. I wondered what I was supposed to do with them.

I brought my mind back to enjoying the extravagant desire people had to treat their canine companions almost like children. This worked very well for me and my natural tendency to enjoy a refined lifestyle, as mentioned earlier. I laid my body on a few pillows, sniffed the fuzzy toys, and glanced at the various T-shirts, boots, collars, leashes and whatnots. I hoped Mom didn't expect me to wear a T-shirt saying Love Bites. Even I had my limits when it came to wearing clothes. I loved my own glossy coat, especially after Johns finished spritzing and fluffing it.

A sales clerk named Karma offered to help Mom who seemed fraught with confusion over what a dog actually required to make a respectable transition into society. About the time I saw Karma reach for a collar with doggie faces on it, I jumped in amidst the turmoil to help make a dignified choice. After all, I would be the one wearing it. Idiot Farmer respected the heritage of his Highland dogs and made sure he threw plaid blankets on a few mounds of hay scattered about the barn in the winter time for us to use as beds. Mom seemed pleased with my ability to coordinate my accessories and somewhat surprised I had an aesthetic penchant for the Tartan plaid. Even I surprised myself sometimes.

Once back at our house, Mom put the large, plaid pillow next to her bed. I noticed her bed was even larger than mine with plenty of room for both of us. I bounced up and down on the mattress a few times and was happy to discover it offered more support than my new pillow. I decided later I would slide myself underneath the covers. I knew I still had the litter mentality where you travel everywhere with your siblings until they no longer have any use for you. People especially struck me as beings who wander aimlessly searching for someone with an irresistible earthy smell that made them want to snuggle up together. Not that I ever saw the farmer and his wife rubbing against each other, but I have seen several people holding hands.

Mom seemed excited over our having a date with a man who suddenly entered her life through the phone. She put on my new collar, changed her clothes, and hurried me back out to the car and then drove to her girly friend's, so he could give me another bath. I wondered if all people spent so much time traveling around in their cars. I began to wonder at what point they stopped using their feet for transportation and began encasing themselves in metal boxes with small windows. The real question in my limited ability to understand this odd species was why they felt the need to make a comfortable place to live and then keep leaving it. If I had a house, I would spend most of my time horsing around the rooms, eating, sleeping, and enjoying the occasional private time to scratch my butt without interruption.

Mom sensed my reluctance to leave again, and so she quieted my nerves with some of Karma's baked goods. Wow, my mouth went into hyper drool over the taste of something that didn't come from a sealed, plastic bag. I ate several more while she put on her lipstick and studied her reflection in the mirror. I heard her sigh with disappointment. She seemed unhappy with her reflection. When Johns held up a mirror in front of my face, I couldn't believe the handsome fellow staring back at me. Hitherto seeing my reflection, I had an image of myself as being something the cat dragged in. Not anymore. I wished Mom could see herself as beautiful as I see her.

Our date went well until HE arrived with the phony smell of an appliance salesman. HE reeked of insincerity. I considered letting go of one of my gaseous toots to discourage any thought he may have about going home with us and sleeping on the big bed, but I didn't want to hurt Mom's feelings, and too, HE might think the foul smell came from her. HE kept looking at me like I needed my manners even more refined, and had the nerve to suggest I become one of his 'dog obedience' students. Suddenly, I could smell the anger coming off of Mom, and the next thing I knew I'm following her back to the car. I figured she was doing us both a favor. I didn't like the sound of the word obedience. I figured out the word leaned toward putting a crimp in my freedom. I mean, from my point of view, wearing a collar curtailed my natural tendency to dawdle over all the odd and irresistible smells. Mom didn't need further pointers on how to keep her new companion in check.

When arriving home Mom kissed the top of my head and, of course, thoughts of Jack came to mind. I wondered where the little guy lived and whether or not his nose had popped back into a proper dog snout. I let these thoughts go as I moseyed into the living room only to discover Mom lying on the couch face down crying like a wounded chicken. I had never seen the farmer's wife cry and so assumed human persons lacked tear ducts and a cache of despairing emotions. I mean, anger had been the only emotion I had seen displayed by the farmer and the over-permed beauty he called his wife. I didn't know exactly what Mom expected me to do to mop up her tears, so I climbed beside her on the couch and tried my best to clean her face with my tongue. She didn't seem to mind and, in fact, started giggling with each heartfelt lick.

Suddenly, she pulled back and regarded me with great affection, and at that moment I knew it was up to me to find a suitable man for us. Yes, definitely, we needed a man who would add another element to our lives instead of infringing upon our freedom, one who likes dogs enough to pamper this one with treats, especially the home-made treats baked at Karma's shop. I knew there must be a man who fell somewhere between the effeminacy of Johns and the over worked, tobacco stained farmer who did not have a clue the ideal man was one with both well-integrated male and female sides. Sometimes, I had no idea what rattled around inside my head, but I knew if I kept my nose to the ground, eventually I would smell the perfect human companion for us.

Fortunately, my new mission did not take long. While bounding through the fields during Mom's preoccupation with her paint brushes, I sniffed an odorous mixture of sweat, calm masculine energy, recently eaten puréed green vegetables, a pocketful of nuts and raisins, and a urine-soaked bush smelling of multivitamins and kelp. I sniffed my way to a strong, healthy male. Perfect, I thought. He smiled, petted me and called me a handsome fellow reinforcing my own opinion when looking into Johns's mirror. I scratched my head and considered ways of dragging his body to Mom without seeming to be obvious about my real intentions. I decided it would be best to work my way into his life with some aplomb before grabbing his arm. Finally, on the second day of watching him clear brush without appearing bored out of my mind, I decided to take action. I barked urgently as though on a rescue mission to get his attention while at the same time I grabbed his hand gently with my teeth and dragged him across the field.

I thought Mom would be pleased, especially since he had offered to share his food with us, but she ran like a jack rabbit being chased by a rambunctious cheetah. I spent the car ride home sulking. I hadn't quite mastered the art of an effective sulk made obvious when I noticed the car kept going until we reached our house and once again encountered the disagreeable noise made by our nosey neighbor. I heard some trumpeting about my needing a job coming from the old codger, when really I considered my job to be taking care of Mom.

3

The tractor painting stood on an easel in my studio still unfinished. Suddenly, I had developed a mental block when trying to render an extra layer of patina on the front fender. My brush wouldn't touch the painting and my hand shook from fear of making a mistake. The painting had become entirely too important as though taking on a life of its own; it had become a difficult, demanding object still waiting for completion. My mind played with this idea until growing tired of the aberration of paranoia. I, personally, had always prided myself on having control of my environment and all the objects in it, so this new development puzzled me, even to the point of becoming anxious, and then suddenly I had an acute awareness of the room's stillness and its feelings of emptiness being almost too much to bear. I realized this is what loneliness must feel like, too much to bear.

I glanced around the studio for Lambert. He sat by the door holding his leash in his mouth with one paw resting on his travel bottle and the other one on my bag of paints. Of course, I knew immediately how he wanted us to spend our day. I just didn't know whether or not Daniel Loggins figured into his agenda. Actually, I knew very little about the inner workings of Lambert's mind and had no idea the extent he would go to get what he thought was best for both of us. I ran my mind over all the reasons why not to drag my painting gear to the countryside, and then suddenly it occurred to me that I really wanted to see Lambert's vegetarian friend again and, in fact, I felt compelled to gather up my brushes, so I could try working on the tractor painting where it had its inception.

Perhaps, the painting would be more cooperative in letting me finish the front fender the exact way in which I had visualized it. I felt better now knowing my mind had complete control over my wobbly desire to abandon the painting altogether and hide underneath the bed covers, except, of course, I had a one woman show next month at the gallery, which handled most of my business.

"Okay, Lambert, let's go," I called after him but he was gone the minute he saw me smiling in his direction. I found him pawing at the back door and trying to shove the dead bolt lock out of position. I mused again over how fortunate I was to have such an intelligent dog. My new companion constantly delighted me with his individual notions of being a dog with a purpose. Naturally, I assumed that purpose meant making himself happy. I had no idea how much he included me in his future plans. Actually, I was so ignorant on how a dog's mind worked that I didn't even know they were capable of having plans.

I mistakenly thought they lived to serve themselves. It embarrasses me to say this, but I really thought all animals served only themselves in a world demanding serious survival skills. I had no idea love entered their world. I studied Lambert staring out the car window and felt the return of peacefulness.

We arrived and went through our familiar routine of setting up our gear most of which had now become Lambert's belongings. He straightened out his cot, arranged his bowls and began to romp in the fields. I positioned my easel in front of the tractor and studied its patina before picking up my brush. My mind settled into a restful stillness for several hours. I loved to paint and felt fortunate I could earn a living at what I do best. I know others think me odd and out of touch, not given to spending long hours on the computer, but instead studying the lines on a leaf through a magnifying glass as though searching for the secret to its beauty. Until Lambert became part of my life, I thought I had it together and functioned better alone than knocking around with friends who encouraged me to get a man, settle down and have a baby. Just listening to my friends describe their daily grind of picking up Junior from playschool, soccer, and all the various clubs designed to keep kids out of trouble, tired my mind and sent me into a feverish state of anxiety fearing someday that would become my life and there would be no time left to paint. I would be lost without a paintbrush in my hand and would then spend my time wondering where I went. I felt smug at being clever enough to avoid the fate that had befallen my friends. My smugness only lasted a short time when I noticed they had become too busy to pencil me into their hectic schedules. And now, except for the grace of Lambert, I felt truly alone.

Even the tractor did not give me comfort, and for the first time I noticed it was an inanimate object left derelict behind a barn. Previous to these unwanted thoughts, I had seen the tractor as an object of beauty. I shoved these invasive thoughts aside and focused on the loveliness of its drooping fender. Then suddenly the tractor's derelict condition became projected onto me, and I saw myself years from now with a broken down body leaning against a barn for support with no one to enliven the spark that had once been me. I shivered from fright. Then Lambert appeared and licked the side of my face while wrapping one arm around my neck. I began to laugh; the joy had returned to distill my imaginary fears.

I glanced up and saw Lambert's vegetarian friend smiling at me. He seemed more handsome today than yesterday. I wondered if that was due to my bout of loneliness and would anyone be a comfort to my loneliness or was this man really what I saw. Yes, I know I spend too much time in my head. I feel better when it is empty.

"Lambert's very persuasive. I hope you have reconsidered having a bowl of chili with me," Daniel said. "I'm ready to break for lunch."

I could not resist his smile and said, "Yes, that would be nice." I kept my desperation under control and pretended the enthusiasm I displayed over the idea of having lunch with someone else to be really about how delicious a bowl of chili would taste. I became excessive in my compliments over a man being able to cook and then when seeing Lambert staring at me with concern, I closed my mouth and quietly returned Daniel's smile.

We walked through a grove of trees along a winding path with Lambert running up ahead like he belonged here. I noticed Daniel wore a flannel shirt today tucked in his blue jeans with a braided leather belt. I'm embarrassed to say I held back a second and studied the shape of his rear and how well it filled out his blue jeans with just the right lift to curve gracefully underneath his back pockets. He turned and waited for me to catch up. Suddenly, I saw a beautiful animated object, all smiles and fluid movements. I realized I had become so distracted by my subject and the idea of putting his blue jeans on canvas, I heard very little of our conversation. I could feel my mouth moving but had no idea what it was saying.

"Heddy, how is your painting of the old tractor coming along?" Daniel asked.

"What?" My mind had ceased working and was lost in thoughts of a man actually being in my bed.

"Your painting of the tractor?" he repeated.

"Oh, yes, well the tractor's painting itself right now." I realized instantly what I had just said must sound idiotic to an earthy, good looking man like Daniel. Even this last observation gave me pause to stop and think about the sudden lack of control over what was now spontaneously coming into my mind, which previously had been kept tighter than a Mason jar. Wayward thoughts were never allowed to disturb the reality I preferred. This new predicament confounded me, left me feeling lost among a plethora of uninvited feelings.

"I know exactly what you mean. When I built this house, it ended up having more rooms than what had been drawn on the blueprints," he responded, still smiling.

We arrived at the end of the path to stand on a tightly woven hill of grass upon which set a beautiful house made of stone and tulip wood.

"Wow!" This time I heard what came out of my mouth and my response startled me.

"I'll take that as a compliment." He laughed and pointed to the copper gutters surrounding a cedar shake roof. "Birds have made their nest in the gutters. I haven't the heart to ask them to leave, so I put a small drain hole in the copper just before their nest to redirect the water. That's why the dangling pipe."

"I didn't notice."

"I think an artist probably notices everything." He glanced at me and smiled. I felt transparent. I wondered if he knew I had already painted his naked body on my imaginary canvas.

"Yes, possibly," I mumbled as we walked inside a stone entry way and then down a slight incline that led to the living room, all sunlight shining on an assortment of well-tended plants including at least four bonsai and a grove of orchids. I looked around to see if he was growing a vegetable garden among the foliage.

"Wow," I said again and now I really felt stupid, like a disoriented interloper into someone else's world that had more definition than my own. Daniel's world consisted of an outward display of beauty and the love of living things. He tended to the garden of nature.

Then suddenly two round couch pillows came to life and stood up to stretch themselves. The pretty faces of the fluffy orange cats possessed a quiet unassuming demeanor of beings who felt comfortable in their own bodies. I would never acquire their equipoise. I would never feel a natural blending of my mind and body. They fought constantly. I found myself making rampant nonsensical comparisons between the real me and my own idealized me. Naturally, the real me fell short. I slumped on a chair opposite the two cats who were now staring at me with sympathetic expressions, as though they understood the sudden awareness of my own shortcomings. This caused me to feel worse. I heard myself groan.

"Heddy, you all right?" Daniel stuck his face in mine and Lambert rested his paw on my knee. I wondered if a person could die of idiocy. If they could, I would probably be dead by now.

"Yes, of course, I'm fine. Just haven't eaten in a while." I glanced down at my shapeless flax ensemble covering a body I hadn't actually noticed in months. I wondered what condition it was in. I went through life exchanging one set of baggy clothes for another. At night I wore flannel pajamas to bed. Once a man enters my life, I feel a sudden need for self-scrutiny.

"Chili just needs heated," my host responded.

"Lovely cats," I said. Daniel and Lambert glanced at the two fur balls now yawning and preparing themselves to curl up again and lie down.

"Oh, yes. They're sisters. Isabel and Philomena."

"How do you tell them apart?"

"Isabel has a white chin and the tip of Philomena's left paw is white." Lambert went over and nosed the two sleeping bodies. They didn't move. He plopped down on the floor and began staring at them as though wondering if he were supposed to be in charge of the two fur objects.

"Lambert's one smart dog. He's gone into herding mode."

"What?"

"Well, he's bred to herd sheep. His own family will naturally come under his charge. He'll feel the need to keep them all in one spot. Fortunately, the kitchen is just off the dining area, so he can still see us while keeping an eye on the cats." Daniel walked into the kitchen with the natural ease of someone who lived there.

My mind flew around the room trying to grab ahold of what he'd just said. We're Lambert's family. I just met this man and all of a sudden I have two sisters named Philomena and Isabel, a man cooking for me and a dog who has it in his head we're his new family. Apparently, I must have been mistaken when thinking Lambert would be happy with just my adoration. I didn't know he felt the need to widen the family circle.

A few minutes later, we sat at the dining room table eating chili out of wooden bowls with red peppers painted on the outside. This enhanced the rustic, down home feeling of his entire house and life style and for a minute I wondered if I had been called in as an extra on a film set, complete with actor husband and an assortment of pets and plants. I felt absorbed into my surroundings and forgot myself for a moment.

"Heddy, you all right?" Daniel asked.

My idiocy embarrassed me and once again I had to assure him of my wellbeing. "Yes, just distracted. I was admiring your home. How lovely. Are you an architect or a farmer?" I asked with all sincerity and was startled when he began to laugh.

"No, neither. I play at farming. I write how to books called *Around the House*. I have to learn everything I write about. So when it translates to my own environment, it only appears that I know my subject really well, when, in fact, I'm actually learning it, while writing it," he said.

"Did you have to become a vegetarian because you wrote a book about it?" I asked in a serious tone. I could feel Lambert's attention shift from his bowl of chili to Daniel. It occurred to me animals would probably feel better in the presence of a vegetarian, somewhat assured they wouldn't end up as the main course on the family dining table.

"No. I've been a vegetarian since I was twelve. I've never been able to stomach the idea of eating animals. I mean, think of it, Heddy, people are putting dead animals in their stomachs. It's not necessary in this country to eat animals except maybe in some parts of Appalachia. Most of us can buy rice and beans at the super market."

Lambert sighed with relief at his end of the table and resumed eating his chili, making very little noise, which I thought odd for someone with a tongue large enough to scoop out the contents of his bowl in one slurp.

"Didn't your parents wonder about you?" Again, I asked with sincerity only to hear Daniel laughing in a manner that sounded like it came from his belly. The laughter shook his entire body.

"Heddy, you are so funny." He laughed some more. I wondered if I should feel insulted. "It's just that your candor is so refreshing. There is certainly no trying to impress me."

"Why would I want to impress you?"

“Because I’m rich. Every time I bring a date into my house, she begins to look for an empty drawer to put her clothes in.”

“Firstly, I didn’t know I was on a date, and secondly I live happily on my own money and don’t need someone else’s.” I stood and threw down my napkin. Lambert hurried to my side as I turned and walked toward the door.

“Heddy, I’m sorry. I was being presumptuous. Can we start over?” he yelled after me.

“We never began, so there’s nothing to start over,” I shot back just before I slammed his hand-carved, oak wood front door with leaded glass windows.

Lambert moseyed back down the winding path emanating sadness. He practically screamed his sadness into my ears, probably so I wouldn’t miss how life had once again become a disappointment to him. I, of course, bore the responsibility of having been the cause of my dog’s disappointment. My ignorance of Lambert’s desire for a family must be so enormous, it would baffle a dog psychologist. I really thought he would be happy with just me as his companion.

“Lambert, would you rather go back to the sheep farm where there are lots of other dogs and sheep?” He licked my hand. I didn’t know how to interpret his response so I asked, “What would you like?” He turned around and began trotting back to Daniel’s house. “Besides living with a misogynist and his two tabbies.” He stopped and I motioned for him to follow me to the car. He resumed sulking and obediently walked alongside me while I gathered up our gear and packed the car. I noticed he let me carry my own bag of paints.

We rode in silence while Lambert stared longingly out the window. His mood filled the car with melancholia the likes of which I hadn't experienced since engaging in conversation with a homeless man who picked over his past dwelling here and there on the highlights of his life's downward spiral into a refrigerator box placed next to a dumpster behind a five star restaurant. I gave him six dollars. This had no effect on his mood, so I gave him ten and then finally when I placed a twenty dollar bill in his hand, he smiled and told me to have a nice day. Later, I saw him passed out next to his box holding an empty bottle of Jack Daniels. I had felt manipulated at the time and wondered if Lambert would be cunning enough to manipulate my feelings into getting his own way. No, I thought, not my Lambert. He would soon snap out of it.

We pulled into the driveway, and I began the process of unpacking the car. He remained seated in the passenger seat with his chin resting on the open window.

"Heddy, yuh dog's not happy. What yuh do to him?" Mr. Dodder appeared suddenly from behind his fence.

"Oh, Mr. Dodder, Lambert will be okay. He just wanted to stay out longer."

"Still not happy. Yuh found decent work fuh him, yet? Herding dog, yuh know. Can't stay idle. Not like them little hair pieces women carry on their arms." Mr. Dodder studied Lambert and shook his head.

"He's just having an off day. Don't dogs have off days, Mr. Dodder?" Now, we both stood staring at Lambert's.

"Well, now, Heddy, there's off days and then there are off days. I'd say Lambert here is suffering the latter," he said and then sighed.

"I'll take him inside and give him a treat. That always cheers him up." I tugged at Lambert's leash until he reluctantly stepped from the car.

I left Mr. Dodder in the driveway shaking his head while I hurried Lambert up the backstairs and inside where I immediately put a treat in his bowl. He walked past it and continued into the living room, climbing upon the couch and putting his head under both paws. I couldn't take it any longer and burst into tears. After all, as I explained to Lambert, I had certain expectations of Daniel, too, and that life wasn't always what we wanted it to be and I might want male human companionship like any other woman. I sat next to him and cried quietly. I could feel him inch his way toward me until we both sat together drowning in our tears and each other's sympathies.

Later we slept together, or at least so I thought until waking up in the middle of the night only to find Lambert missing from his half the bed. I called for him but nothing. I crept around the house looking in all the logical places until coming to the kitchen where I discovered the back door was open. I stepped outside and noticed the latch on the gate had been unlocked and it, too, stood open. I grabbed an old raincoat and ran outside with my flashlight looking for Lambert.

My heart pounded in my chest and for a second I couldn't breathe. Panic had overtaken me. Life without Lambert loomed before me, a lonely life without his loving glance and warm fur. Tears welled in my eyes and streamed down my face. I leaned against the fence to pull myself together when hearing a familiar voice.

"Heddy, got yuh dog here. Found him pacing in front of yuh house." Mr. Dodder held Lambert by a rope he had attached to his collar. He gave it to me and even in the moonlight I could see a disapproving scowl come across my neighbor's face.

I tried to sound casual. "Oh, he probably just decided to go for a midnight ramble. Right, Lambert?" Lambert's tail fell between his legs as he pulled away from me and walked through the gate and up the stairs to open the screen door with his paw.

"Well, got yuhself a roamer. Yupsee doodle dee. A real roamer, that one. Don't get him a job soon, Heddy, yuh gunna wake up and find him missing fuh good."

"Thank you, Mister Dodder," I called after him. I made a mental note to put more locks on my doors.

I spent the better part of the night wondering if I had been too hasty in leaving Daniel with my half-eaten bowl of chili and a few harsh words. After all, he was a man with an ego and maybe his ego bruised easily from previous hurts. How would I know what lay beneath his beautiful, self-important exterior if I did not dare to look any further than a few unfortunate words? I turned these thoughts over in my mind and added a few more to further confuse my self-righteous attitude toward the male of our species. I had no idea why I felt this way. My father possessed a fervent desire to live life full tilt until falling off a mountain when rock climbing with his friends. My mother had died of heart break from the loss a year later on the very day of my eighteenth birthday. She sent a few mixed messages by baking my cake first with the words, 'Happy Birthday and Good bye to my baby girl' written in pink icing. Upon reading these words, I hurried to her bedroom where I found her unconscious body. She died on the way to the hospital of cardiac arrest.

My parents had been considerate in not making me suffer the long, lingering illnesses of most aged parents. They died while still in their forties without giving me the opportunity to watch their faces become lined from the passing of time. I still missed their laughter. I used to glide on the waves of their laughter. Their laughter gave joy to the first half of my life and now here I lay in bed, wondering where I went wrong to end up alone and a sorry disappointment to a dog I barely knew but loved.

The next morning I put Lambert's leash on him and led him to the car. He scrambled in the passenger seat and let me buckle him with his harness. I don't know where he thought we were going, but a few minutes later we arrived at Karma's store. I asked her for something to calm Lambert's nerves after relating the incident with Daniel and adding how upset Lambert was with me because he had chosen a permanent home for the two of us with Daniel and the two bookends he called cats, and the jungle he was growing in the living room, and not to mention the biggest ego I have ever had to endure on any of my dubious dates. I recounted all this with my hands flying through the air for emphasis and Lambert laying on one of the large dog pillows he had pulled off the shelf for himself. I could tell he had settled himself in for the long haul of my monologue covering life's injustices and the impossible task of finding a good man who met all my expectations. My mind scurried about in this manner for some time.

"Calm down, Heddy." Karma said in her sweet and soothing voice. "I think you're the one who needs something for your nerves. I would suggest Rescue Remedy." She showed me several rows of small yellow boxes called Bach Flower Essence.

"Me! There's nothing wrong with me so long as the rest of mankind acts well socialized. It's not every day I'm sitting at the table of someone I perceive as enjoyable company without thoughts of fitting him into my calendar until I die. But that was his presumption. Imagine, having a man think you were eating his chili because you saw yourself living rich on a back road in the middle of nowhere? I don't know who he's been dating, probably some writer from *Town and Country* magazine, no doubt."

"Maybe you better just take the Rescue Remedy full strength. Here take the entire eyedropper." Karma stuck the glass dropper in my mouth and squeezed the second I was about to open it and let go of another litany of complaints. A few minutes later, I felt somewhat calm and in control of my runaway words.

Karma then led me through a doorway of hanging beads and sat me down on a bean bag that had been upholstered in a heavy cotton design of a Picasso painting from his cubistic period, a veritable patchwork of eyes and noses. I became completely engrossed trying to figure out what went where, not realizing the remedy had taken effect, and I now felt at ease despite only being six inches from the floor. I have never been a floor person, one of those people who are comfortable crawling around on the floor while you're trying to have a normal, grown up conversation with them only to be distracted by their bird-like poses. Karma interrupted this image.

"Feel better?" she asked but went on before I had a chance to respond. "You know, Heddy, that's zero for two."

"What are you talking about, baseball?"

"I'm talking about your abysmal dating record inside of a week. You went out with two really nice men and rejected both of them, because you thought they wanted something from you that didn't fit in with your own preconceived notions of how an hour of your time should be spent."

"You'll have to admit that Randall character had an opportunistic motive in wanting me to engage him as Lambert's trainer." Just then I noticed Lambert lying across from me on his own bean bag. Despite being upset with me, his herding instinct kicked in and caused him to be protective. I softened.

"You don't know much about men, Heddy. That was probably just an opening. He knew you by name and really appreciated your art work." Karma smiled sweetly.

"Oh, and that's supposed to make me feel better? The man wanted to meet me because he likes my paintings!"

"Well, would you rather he wanted you for your body?"

"I haven't seen my body in ages." I glanced down at my uniform flax ensemble and sighed. Lambert felt my pain and sighed, too. Now, I knew he couldn't hold a grudge. I leaned over and stroked him until he closed his eyes.

"Yes, you don't really dress to attract a man." Karma wore a pair of blue jeans, fitted white shirt and two loopy turquoise necklaces around her neck, with lovely long gray hair pulled back and a flawless complexion emphasized with soft red lipstick. I could never pull off that look, and I'm at least twenty years younger. I realized at that moment age had nothing to do with style. The woman definitely had style.

"I know. I'm probably too fat for one."

"How would you know underneath all that material? I'll bet you wear flannel to bed."

I laughed so hard, I nearly fell out of my bean bag. Karma smiled and the next thing I knew we are out the door and on the way to her favorite boutique for women. Lambert sat in the display window among the stuffed animals and stared at us with his face pressed against the glass until we disappeared a few blocks down the street.

We ransacked the boutique for what seemed hours. I found the racks of clothes overwhelming in their demanding a decision needed to be made on my size and lifestyle. I had no clue about my lifestyle once Lambert had been added to my list of daily activities.

"See how impossible it is to shop for me?" I told Karma.

"We've only been here fifteen minutes." Karma held up a russet colored silk shirt. "This would look nice with your dark red hair and freckles."

"I always thought my hair was blah brown. That's why I have it highlighted."

"No. With your hair and lifestyle you're definitely a Capri-cargo with tucked in silk blouse type girl, which you can vary on long walks with Lambert by wearing a lightweight flannel shirt and braided leather belt. This will turn you from baggy slouch to country chic in five minutes. Plus, we'll stop at my favorite shoe store and find a pair of Ferragamo moccasins for going out and tie-up ankle boots for walking."

"What's that?" I noticed Karma's bundle of clothes draped over her arm.

"We have to determine your size first and then start whittling down the pile to get you started." She hurried toward the dressing room, and I followed feeling like a six year old shopping for school clothes with her mother.

When I stepped in front of the three way mirror, Karma laughed with pleasure. "See, look at what a cute body you have and didn't know it."

I glanced in the mirror and noticed my stomach was missing and the fat roll on my hips had disappeared along with a couple of inches from my waist. I fit neatly into the mid-calf khaki pants and silk blouse. My hair, did indeed, pick up the color from the blouse making it appear more red than auburn. Even my freckles seemed attractive in a girlish sort of way. I could feel my mood lift from underneath all that flax now discarded on the dressing room floor.

"Look, you really are a hot little number. Men like to see a woman's silhouette and not the store dummy dressed in a couple of empty feed sacks."

I admired myself for another minute before growing bored with my reflection. I allowed Karma to gather up three outfits in the same size and use my credit card to pay for them. Next, she rummaged through a hundred pairs of shoes before settling on the perfect pair of moccasins and brown tie-up ankle boots along with a wad of knee hi argyle socks. I expected her to duplicate her own style when dressing me, but she definitely possessed an objective eye when it came to another person's aesthetics. I thanked her profusely, threw my boxes in the car and then ran to retrieve Lambert who was still sitting with his nose pressed against the glass window.

"Lambert, come here boy. I missed you terribly." I called to him, but he flew to my side just as I held out my arms to hug him. I then realized we had not been separated since he arrived in my life. I had never been in a codependent relationship before but could feel myself being pulled in by the gentle tugs of my new dog's heart strings. I smiled to myself and suddenly life seemed to be full of boundless possibilities and the loveliness of a nearly well-lived life.

4

LAMBERT WEIGHTS IN:

I settled in with Mom and didn't mind the paint smells coming from her studio where she worked when not in the fields finding some kind of fascination with old tractors and barns. I never quite got used to smelling like a perfumed hooker so spent as much time as possible rolling around in all the pungent odors coming naturally off the grassy knolls around the barn where Mom sat slapping several coats of paint on a square canvas. She could spend hours in this activity, which quite frankly would bore my hairy butt after about fifteen minutes. Fortunately, she became engrossed with her paint set to the point of forgetting about my comings and goings altogether. This suited me fine because, even though, I am not actively working as a herding dog, I still liked a good romp through the meadows.

I found endless delight in scattering the crows pecking along the ground. Crows have always been considered an aggravation to a newly sown cornfield. Being lazy birds, they look around their hometown for the nearest garden and spend the early morning hours pecking at the dry seeds then fly to the nearest tree and idle away the rest of the day happily belching fumes from a full stomach. I have always felt sorry for the gardeners who only wanted to till their own soil and enjoy the fruits of their labor or the ones who sold them at all the vegetable stands for extra money. Yes, the crow cackles over being the bane of the gardener's existence, an irritating sound that annoys the ears of even the deafest old plodder. If dogs could fly, there would be a lot fewer crows cluttering up our landscape.

Sometimes, during my bucolic romping, I took a moment to reflect on my early memories with siblings, wondering what happened to them. I found myself hoping they managed to be relocated to a dog lover's house and not have to stay where they would spend their lives trampling through sheep manure and thorny bushes to get at some wayward sheep only valued for its wool. I sighed at these memories.

I remembered nearly drowning in the bucket of milk where Idiot Farmer threw our tiny bodies. First born brother had struggled to get me out of the bucket. He jumped back in when noticing I wasn't among the others shaking the milk from their fur onto the barn floor. He dove in the milk and came up under me to push my tiny butt with his head. He then spent an hour helping me get the milk from my fur. Occasionally, while on these sojourns into the past, tears would drop from my eyes at the fate of my heroic, older brother. I could not help but wonder what had befallen him. My mind may have a limited grasp of such concepts as fate and destiny, but I know when a dog's feet smell of manure, you can bet his life is similarly imbued. Yes, indeed, life sucked for most farm dogs.

Eventually though, I pulled myself from these doldrums by looking about my surroundings for a good distraction. That was when I stumbled onto the Happy Herbivore. I could see his teeth from a hundred yards where he sat smiling on a log. I could tell he liked the idea of doing a good day's work on his farmette, and I liked the idea he didn't feel the need to kill animals and eat them. It made me feel safe. I watched him for a while before deciding to take him to meet Mom. After her last disaster with a human male, I wanted to make sure the Happy Herbivore would be as kind to her as he was to animals.

HH sat in the sunshine smiling at nothing in particular. I supposed most people would think he resembled a simpleton. I noticed in my short life that others resented happiness where it did not belong. Happiness in human society seemed to be connected to team sports. Yes, I saw humans yesterday standing in front of Ted's TV store watching a baseball game and jumping up and down when their favorite athlete hit the ball. Yet, these same people might look at HH happily doing nothing and consider him simple minded. I wondered about their logic. I considered it suspect and worthy of occasional thought. HH appeared not to care what others thought of him, probably because he assumed no one was watching, not even a dog hiding in the bushes. He was so comfortable while feeling alone in the woods that he farted, a loud toot requiring him to lift one buttock to let the noise escape. Mom would never approve of a man farting or a dog for that matter especially one she considered to be her perfect companion in a world of imperfect males. I have to keep my own farts from flying out my butt and filling the air with noxious fumes common to dogs who are adjusting to a new diet. Sometimes, when I felt one tumbling down my inner tract, I shoved my butt against the nearest wall and stopped breathing. Usually, this did the trick, and then I excused myself and went to another room and let loose. If I had free rein of the yard, I could do all my business outside in a normal manner underneath the sky.

I don't understand a human's need to live in an elaborate over-decorated wooden box. The other day I had trouble making myself comfortable in Mom's bed because she had a dozen throw pillows piled on top to make it look like some woman's bed by the name of Martha Stewart. Who is this Martha Stewart person and why does she have a hold on Mom's need to copy what this decorous person has to say? I mean, I know she's an ex-con, so why do girl humans listen to her advice on throw pillows? I mean, did she have her cell full of throw pillows and were her cell walls painted designer colors? If a dog engages in an illegal activity, you bet he'll find his butt in the nearest pound, which is far worse than a jail cell. At least humans get a trial before they are executed. Not so with dogs.

I know these things because I talk incessantly to the dogs walking along the street. Humans have no idea of our ability to communicate without making a lot of noise with the language. Words don't have to come out of our mouths to reach another dog's ears or any animal for that matter. No, I can tune in to the dog grapevine and find out whatever I want to know. For instance, I know right now Jack from the vet's office is having bacon and eggs for breakfast. He'll be farting all day from eating something that doesn't belong in anybody's stomach and then Jack will get on the dog grapevine and complain about the stomach ache he has to suffer while his Mom lives in Wonderland believing herself the perfect mother for catering to Jack's stomach in a human fashion obsessed with the whole breakfast regime. Yesterday, he complained about the pancakes piled on his plate. I told him, "Hey buddy, ya gotta stop eatin' the stuff 'cause it's gonna kill ya." He just sniveled a little bit and then dove once again into his Mom's purse looking for an antacid pill. Jack's a resourceful little bastard; I'll give him that.

But my thoughts have strayed from the human subject. HH has now begun eating his berries and nuts from a small biodegradable bag. No shit, the guy's perfect for Mom and me. He probably chops his own wood for the fireplace and cans the vegetables from his garden if the crows haven't eaten his seeds, and I feel certain there's a compost heap somewhere near his backdoor.

HH stood to cut some more brush from underneath the trees. He took a few swipes before wiping the sweat off his forehead with a red bandanna. I hoped Mom wouldn't think his behavior with the hanky too female. But then upon further reflection, I remembered the girly man who gave me weekly shampoos and dismissed this thought. Any truck stop waitress would appear more masculine than her high-pitched, twitchy man friend. So I thought maybe all the fluttering around with the hanky might be a good thing to Mom if she feels more comfortable with soft males.

I continued to observe the prospect I was about to drag out of the woods to be Mom's future mate. He was studying all the underbrush he had just whacked off as though not knowing what to do with it. Idiot Farmer always piled it up somewhere and let the sheep eat the leaves off the bushes before setting fire to the dry branches. I would be a wealth of farm information if humans had the wherewithal to tune into the dog grapevine.

He neatened the pile and then tied it in small bundles, which made all the branches appear more manageable, and then he put these bundles in a bright and shiny wagon behind a bright and shiny what appeared to be a replica of Idiot Farmer's tractor. Not a speck of dirt anywhere. Even the mud flaps hung daintily from the back fenders. HH wouldn't last a day on a working farm. The farm hands ate with their fingers between wrestling the sheep for shearing and digging a thousand acres of post holes with a double shovel. I never saw any of them mop up their sweat with a hanky. Nope. They just ran their foreheads up their flannel sleeves once in a while and kept moving. One thing though, they farted as freely as a sheep with a gassy stomach. Mom sure wouldn't want a farm hand in her bed. He'd be snoring before his head hit one of her decorator pillows. Nope. I happily concluded HH the faux farmer might be the perfect metro- male for Mom's delicate sensibilities and artistic temperament.

Actually, though, Mom seemed to react more strongly to the words that came out of a man's mouth than his appearance. She complained for two days about the dog trainer being a dolt for intimating she might want to hire him to help with my obedience training. I didn't remember him saying exactly all the things she had heard, but then I noticed humans rarely say what they mean and some don't mean what they say. So poor Mom, no wonder she had trouble tiptoeing through the mind field of dating communication. Dogs don't bother with all the preliminaries of dating. If a female doesn't want you slobbering all over her, she just bites you and then runs like hell. No mixed messages between genders in our species. Most males feel fortunate to have their balls left intact after one of these skirmishes. It embarrasses me to confess I am still a virgin in that department but have no doubt my day will come if Maggie the Butcher doesn't have a go at my balls first.

HH finished loading all of his branch bundles into the back of the shiny wagon and then stood silently for a moment to admire the neatness of his handiwork. I noticed it didn't take much to please him, which worked in his favor so far as I'm concerned, because Mom couldn't really cook and hired her housework done by a large woman with an annoying accent. She sounded like a general bossing around a small army when she walked in the door and found me loitering in the kitchen, dropping crumbs near my food bowl. I could tell the second she picked up her dust rag and bore down on anything resembling misplaced dirt, the dust mites wouldn't dare come out of their hiding places for fear of dying a slow and painful death. No, Mom definitely wasn't handy so the Happy Herbivore's tendency to twitter over his own small accomplishments would make him a perfect mate.

I decided to grab his arm before he climbed onto his junior tractor and took off. He seemed startled when seeing me latched onto the end of it, but he still smiled and didn't smell like fear, not that I was a danger to his wellbeing, but a male does like to be perceived as being a menace. Even metro-males must want to appear dangerous underneath all their hair products.

I pulled HH along to Mom on the other side of the barn. Occasionally, I let go and barked with the urgent pleadings of a rescue dog. I outdid myself when pointing my snout in the direction of Mom blissfully splattering paint on her canvas. Finally, I presented him to her and stood back to be thanked for my find, but she looked at him like he was something the cat dragged in. I knew the feeling, of course, and felt sorry for HH who I noticed stood there smiling and probably expecting to be appreciated for arriving suddenly into her life. This would definitely work against him. Mom may have wanted a man in her life but she wasn't desperate enough to settle for a lackluster soul mate.

I began drooling when he asked us to his house for chili. I practically soaked the ground with my drool over the thought of sucking up some hearty homemade soup. My own food bowl contained factory kibble hard enough to break a tooth. Mom mumbled several words and then gathered up her canvas and ran to our car. I studied HH for a second to see if I had misjudged his appearance. No, he looked pleasant and Mom hadn't even bothered to check him for fleas, so neither one of the males she left behind possessed a clue on her sudden departure. Naturally being a loyal companion, I eventually followed Mom to the car carrying her paint bag, but my heart sank that day, and I sulked all the way home. Who knew what humans wanted in their small, wooden box houses or could even tolerate living with them.

The old codger next door got in a few pot shots before we could high tail it into the house, still pushing that nonsense about my getting a proper job. I could tell his laconic tongue flapping at Mom was beginning to wear thin. She mentioned something about giving him framing work. This would fix him. I could tell he'd rather annoy other people with his bright ideas than use them himself. I noticed he spent most of the day playing with his truck and sunning in the backyard while whittling pieces of wood into birds, ducks mostly. I could see him out the window whenever I walked upstairs to get a drink from the toilet.

Mom seemed disgusted over my preferring the water in the big bowl rather than the bottled stuff she poured in my metal bowl. Truth be told, most dogs would rather lap up the cool water in a porcelain bowl where there is plenty of head room than try to sip it from a tin cup.

Dogs in general have been taken out of context. Our ancestors scooted about the wilds trying to keep a low profile, scrounging for food and drinking water from the nearest riparian water supply. Now, we wear fancy collars, have our hair done, our nails manicured, and travel at the side of a human person who is afraid to be alone. Several centuries of adjustment have brought about our new status, but occasionally one of the human persons sticks his nose where it doesn't belong and upsets the delicate balance most of us have going.

The old codger spent entirely too much time muddling over my work life. Even I enjoyed a lazy day now and again and wouldn't want to be tied to the daily grind of repeating the same task until my easy going disposition turned snarly, causing me to bite the nearest moving thing that aggravated my already disheveled nerves. Nope. The old codger had gotten himself so far up my hairy butt, he could bark for me. I made a mental note to chomp on a few of his cherished ducks the next time he was given to organizing my life.

Meanwhile, Mom changed her mind about eating HH's chili, even asking me my opinion, which I would readily give to her if she had an inkling as to how to tune into my thoughts. Human persons while limited, jabber noisily about their feelings and then sigh with resignation when not getting wordy feedback from their canine companions. If I ever met one of those animal communicators Jack waxes on about, I would have certainly given her a mouthful of opinions she could pass along to Mom.

The next day we found ourselves walking peacefully along a winding path to HH's house. I could smell greenhouse flowers, warm chili, a few chickens, and flea prevention odors coming from two felines, not to mention, a few obnoxious odors wafting from a small barn, housing an unhappy horse named Thomas Jefferson. His sadness affected my good mood and even when I asked him about his low spirits, he said he didn't want to talk about it. I turned my attention back to the smell of chili and forgot the horse altogether once I found my nose buried in cat hair. The lazy fur balls draped on the couch would make me look like a workaholic in the eyes of the old codger. I briefly wondered what would be suitable employment for something that looked like a winter muff.

Despite the perplexity over their general uselessness, I still felt compelled to sit next to the furry hand warmers in herding dog pose. This bored my butt. I really wanted to check out the indoor garden, sniff a few plants, and investigate the house for other interesting smells. The only thing of mildly odorous interest rested on the coffee table in a tiny cage with straw on the bottom. It resembled a large mouse. In an effort to shove my nose closer I accidently opened the tiny cage door. Next thing I know I got the sucker clamped to my snout with the force of a badger in heat. I tried shaking the thing loose, but it had ground its teeth so far into my honker, I could hear myself groan from the pain. The ruckus woke up the two fur balls who promptly went to town on the rodent yanking it with such ferocity, the thing flew through the air and landed in a large clay pot where it clamored to get out. I could hear my new feline BFFs titter over its predicament and then as quickly as they had rallied, they slipped back into their coma. I glanced at them fondly and decided maybe they actually might have a purpose in the bustle of the work a day world. I sat happily next to them and ignored all the squeaking going on in the clay pot.

I turned my attention to the kitchen where Mom and HH stood at the stove trying to determine the degree of heat needed to make a perfect bowl of chili. I would eat the stuff cold. My taste buds lacked all discrimination and leaned toward the gourmand side rather than suffering from any gourmet indulgences. Nope. I would eat a bowl of oats without milk and cinnamon, and you wouldn't hear nary a complaint coming from this lackadaisical herding dog.

While just sitting there protecting the hand warmers, I decided to check out my balls to make sure they were nice and tidy, no pee stains running down the undercarriage. Mom didn't appreciate any unpleasantness coming from the area of my animal zoo, so I spent a few seconds every day making sure to keep it ship shape. I don't know why dogs tend to be fond of their own balls. Jack got on the grapevine and told the entire dog population about the nervous breakdown he had over the loss of his. You can't help but feel sorry for the little bastard, makes him seem like less of a real dog and more of an arm ornament for his mom. Jack cried to everyone who had the patience to listen to his diatribe on Maggie the Butcher leaving him with nothing but three stitches and a band aid. Said life would never be the same and something about his options being limited. We all knew Jack's options of having a family with the same said mom who gave the go ahead to have his balls removed, would never allow him to father a litter of little Jacks needing to be fed. Nope. She liked her little guy sans family. She wanted him all to herself for company. If she could hear him run off at the mouth though, she might not find him such companionable company and give him the option of finding his way from her front door to the streets. He wouldn't last an hour in a suburb, much less living the life of a back alley cur.

Finally, Mom and HH brought the chili to the dining table where I made myself at home in the Captain's chair. Both glanced in my direction but said nothing. I knew HH had to be on his best behavior if he wanted to impress Mom and yelling at her dog to get down from the table wouldn't be in his best interest. And since Mom had never had a dog in her life until my arrival, I knew enough to affect a breezy air about fitting myself into the family picture in order to make my presence appear normal. HH, after serving Mom, placed a large bowl on my place mat. I waited for the human diners to daintily pick up their spoons and begin eating before I shoveled the stuff in my mouth with the curled end of my tongue. I lapped my bowl clean inside of thirty seconds, restrained a belched and slipped off the Captain's chair and back to my post.

I settled myself for an afternoon nap, but seconds later I heard the sounds of Mom's voice going on about some indignity HH had committed with a few wayward words. He said something about women getting into his drawers. This didn't sound like Mom. She kept so much to herself, she would have no idea everybody else's stuff overlapped and sometimes ended up in someone else's drawers. She never misplaced anything and from the words I could get ahold of HH had blundered into one of Mom's personal landmines and blown up all his good intentions of wanting to make her happy with his homemade chili. Poor bastard, reminded me of Jack, always left wondering exactly what he had done to deserve being in such a predicament.

Needless to say, my own fantasies of Mom and me nestled cozily on HH's farmette had been demolished with a few words, no doubt, a misunderstanding of some sort between human persons. I began to wonder how much of a grasp Mom had of her own language. I mean other than a bowl of chili what could she expect from a man who lived with two cats, a sad horse, and a rodent? He was bound to have a few rough edges in need of smoothing. Her unwillingness to overlook his bungling the language indicated a lack of tolerance for the human male on Mom's part.

She hustled my hairy butt right out the front door and down the winding path. I put up some resistance by sulking all the way home, but Mom sat sunk in her own disappointment and paid little attention to mine. Once home, I piled myself on the couch for a good cry. Finally, she noticed and came over to comfort me. We both cried together with lots of noisy sup supping and a string of words coming from Mom on their not being any nice men left for her to sort through. I wondered where they had all gone.

"Yes, Lambert, you wouldn't believe what I've had to endure on endless dates with these Neanderthals. Once a man brought his medical records on our first date, wanted to show me what a healthy specimen he was and how his children would be perfect if I were interested in taking him seriously as a future husband. And another time, a man brought his mother with him, a large battle axe with a lazy eye and a sharp tongue. Kept calling me dearie. Oh, and another time too embarrassing to mention, which I know of course you won't, but a man asked me to take a look at his large penis. He thought it was a selling point. Needless to say Lambert, I thought he was a pervert. And now I'm not even date worthy because I'm super sensitive to what even a nice man would say, and maybe I over reacted when walking out on Daniel like that but who knows what lurks inside his vegetable bin."

She lost me on her date with the large penis. My mind had to switch gears to imagine this happening in the canine world. A dog's penis is definitely not a selling point for female dogs. No, they would find us too disgusting to take seriously if we felt the urge to show off our animal parts before getting down to business. Most of us kept them tucked up nice and neat behind a few sprouts of hair. Nope, definitely not something we dogs strutted in plain sight. Besides that, if a bitch saw one out of context, she would snap the thing in two with a sharp pair of incisors.

The next day I found myself scrunched into a bean bag listening to Mom recount her experiences with Daniel to the boutique lady, where I knew she hoped to find a sympathetic ear. Now you may have noticed, I have been completely indifferent to the Santa Fe Senior but this time she impressed me with her lack of sympathy. I mistakenly assumed she would chime in and sing along with Mom's lengthy lament on the shortcomings of men. No sirree Bob, the Santa Fe Senior told her in no uncertain terms to pull herself up by her bootstraps and get out there and try again. She told Mom she hadn't given the last two men a chance to make up for their carelessness with the English language, which is exactly what I thought, except as mentioned earlier, I couldn't help Mom with any of my pithy insights due to her disadvantaged communication skills with animals.

Mom protested and seemed somewhat taken aback at her new BFF's lack of sympathy. I'm sure she thought a woman her age would have experienced the seedy side of dating and come out with a frayed nervous system on the subject of men. Wrong. Santa Fe Senior gave Mom a good tongue lashing on her manner of dress, said she lacked style and her clothes looked like the burlap sacks found at a feed and grain store and no man had enough imagination to visualize the loveliness underneath. I, on the other hand, liked the smell of flax and enjoyed nuzzling against Mom's baggy britches. Nobody asked me, though, and, in fact, the two of them left me with a bunch of stuffed dummies looking simple in the store window. Set me back some worrying over whether or not Mom had disappeared altogether, and wondering who would fill my food bowl if she never returned to claim her cherished companion. My imagination took flight and left me to whimper over all kinds of fears, including an empty toilet bowl. What would I do for water? I took a few minutes to scour the place, check out the water and food supply. I located an entire rack of gourmet treats for spoiled dogs, Jack came to mind here, and enough water to hole up for the duration. I then wandered back to the window and waited along with the dummy dogs, which were an embarrassment to my species. I mean a purple Dachshund.

Finally, Mom returned wearing a fancy pair of slippers and some heavy cotton pants with her ankles showing. She was smiling. I sighed with relief when noticing she wasn't laden with turquoise and silver bobbles like her new girlfriend. She shoved me into the car with her packages, and we hurried home to sit next to the phone. I had no idea why.

I thought my day couldn't get any more exhausting until hearing the sounds of the old codger come flying across the fence. He kept running at the mouth over my getting a proper job and something about my being a problem dog and ending up in Juvi. I may have imagined that last bit but at least that's the general gist of what the old busybody kept shouting in Mom's ear. Said I needed to be on anti-depressants, and that I'd probably end up too sad to be of use to anybody unless Mom put me out to work in some pasture guarding a bunch of grubby sheep. My own nerves had taken a beating that day, and all I wanted to do was find my bed and lie down in it. Later, I would go for an evening walk in hopes of reconnecting with mother moon. I always found solace in the comfort of nature, so long as I didn't have to get my feet dirty and worry about fleas housing themselves in my fur, as mentioned earlier.

5

I studied my new wardrobe with doubts when throwing the 'new me' on the bed, matching tops and bottoms along with appropriate shoes. I loved my old, baggy, lived-in clothes where the air could blow underneath and wrap around my legs keeping them cool on a warm day. I realized that feeling of comfort would be too hard to explain to Karma, a woman who placed more value on style than comfort. I sighed over my new clothes but was determined to wear them when gadding about the countryside looking for inspiration.

Daniel came to mind again, and I could feel a few tears well in my eyes and threaten to roll down my cheeks in an expression of sadness over my dismantled love life. Yes, even I had to admit my efforts to work a man into my life had failed miserably. My efforts had been trampled under the heels of my new boots. I sat down on the bed and let go of the tears staggering to remain silent. Lambert jumped up beside me, and then suddenly I couldn't hold it any longer and buried my face in his warm fur and cried like life couldn't get any worse. But I knew differently. Life from an objective point of view couldn't get much better for a person who appreciated the gift of expression. Yes, I had been blessed with the freedom to express myself on canvas and paid well for the satisfaction it gave to me.

Lambert nuzzled closer, trying to absorb my grief. His new presence in my life made me feel more like a fool for crying over what I didn't have and not appreciating all the beauty in my life. How had I ever managed without his loving ways and yes, why couldn't he be the man I thought I wanted but couldn't seem to fit into the narrow zone I had carved out for one? While sniffling on his fur, I noticed a tiny sore spot. Immediately, I forgot Daniel and picked up the phone to call Maggie for an emergency appointment.

"Two o'clock but that's three hours from now. What if it's a fast moving infection or some skin disease in need of immediate treatment? Maybe it hurts and he needs a pain killer. Can't I come now? Oh, thank you."

I put Lambert's leash and collar on him, told him not to worry, that Maggie would find a cure, and hurried us to the car passing Mr. Dodder so fast he didn't have time to form a short sentence. We arrived ten minutes later and sat in the waiting room with that funny little Pug and his mother. Lambert seemed distracted by his presence and left my side to go stick his nose against the little dog's flat face. They licked each other like they had been friends for life. I wondered why people couldn't be this friendly, and then remembered I wasn't exactly warm and fuzzy when it came to social interactions. The dog's mother smiled at me like aren't they just the cutest things. She possessed a sunny disposition that made me suspect she might be on pills. I never believed people just naturally went around smiling all day. Life surely must get them down some time and when it did, they popped a pill or found solace in a stiff drink.

The woman introduced herself, "Hi, I'm Sally and this is my dog Jack." Now, I wondered if we were supposed to bond similar to our dogs. This troubling prospect annoyed me. I just wanted to be left alone to mull over my thoughts, feel sorry for myself, and worry about Lambert having leprosy.

"Hi. I'm Heddy and this is Lambert, who your dog has already met the last time we were here," I said in a cordial manner that surprised even me. Lambert and his friend continued to find each other fascinating for some reason.

"Why are you here?" she asked and suddenly I felt my comfort zone shrink to a half an inch around the soles of my shoes.

"Lambert has a sore on his back," I responded. Sally pulled her dog away from Lambert's nose and checked Jack's fur for signs of a devastating skin disease.

"I don't think it's contagious. He probably caught it on a bramble bush. We've been out in the woods recently," I assured her and noticed she relaxed the grip on Jack. The word neurotic came to mind, but I quickly realized it could also apply to my own behavior and decided to let that line of thinking alone. Instead, I turned and smiled at her. Just then the receptionist called for Jack, and they vanished behind the exam room door.

I noticed a man sitting across from us. Usually men don't flirt with me, so I figured he must be responding to my new clothes. I wore the leather braided belt, which accented a small waist and had part of my calf showing below the Capri pants when crossing my legs. I watched his eyes run up and down my clothes as though I were the dummy in a department store window. Finally, his eyes came to rest on my face, and he smiled but his smile was too late to enamor me with a set of white teeth and an overzealous interest in my body. His smile had already turned into a leer and caused me to sit uncomfortably in a hard back chair, worrying about his eyeballs traveling inside my clothing.

"Nice looking dog, you have there. I'll bet he gives you a run for your money. Herding dogs have a quiet nobility about them. I'm a faculty member at Harvard. We study dogs and their relationships to man. Credit has been given to them for saving our species from extinction by eating the meat our ancient ancestors left on the bones of the animal carcasses lying next to their beds."

"You don't say." My eyes glazed over with boredom. I wished Jack would hurry and finish his exam. I just wanted this man to shut up and leave me in peace to worry over Lambert's sore spot. I knew I was supposed to be impressed by his credentials but nothing in what he had just said indicated a love of dogs. A cat lay next to him across a chair and fiddled with her own leash. Actually, I found her more fascinating than her owner. She hung her head upside down and stared at Lambert, even held out her paws. Nothing about her languid posture suggested any feelings of fear. I found myself envying her. Lambert went over and licked her face and then stuck his own face next to her owner's ear and growled.

"Your dog's displaying territorial behavior. He doesn't want me talking to his mistress."

I wondered if this man would ever shut up, and why suddenly he found me a willing receptacle to his dog knowledge. "I've never seen him do that before. Usually, Lambert prefers to observe people rather than to get directly involved with them," I said before realizing how insane that nonsense sounded. The man laughed.

"Yes, well, a herding dog would be a keen observer. This one obviously takes his job seriously when it comes to protecting his litter."

"His litter?" I never thought of myself as part of Lambert's litter.

"Yes, a lot of people sleep with their dogs, eat with them, play endless games with them, and then wonder why their dogs treat them like litter mates. It's a current theory held by animal behaviorists."

"I guess you keep your dog staked to a small house in the backyard," I responded before I could censor my thoughts. I fully expected a harsh comeback, but he laughed again.

"I'm John Hornbach, full professor in the biology department, behavioral genetics. Feel free to call my secretary and come see me. I would love to take you on a tour of our facilities. Bring your dog." He said this as though believing I would be honored to go to his lab and take a peek at all the dogs laboring in control groups. I briefly considered stepping outside for some fresh air when the exam room door opened where Jack bounded off the metal table and shoved himself under Lambert.

"Fifi, you're next." A technician called and Professor Hornbach stood and again smiled at me while proffering a business card. Lambert growled in a low voice. The Professor just laughed and disappeared into the small room recently vacated by Jack. I could feel chills run up my back and for a moment I thought of Daniel. I missed his easy going nature and sweet smile. I tossed the professor's business card in the wicker trash basket next to my chair.

My thoughts came to an abrupt halt when noticing Lambert and Jack were now wrestling together on the floor. Jack kept trying to get closer to Lambert and even barked when Sally reached down to connect his leash to his collar. Then suddenly Lambert rolled over the small dog and tucked him up against his underside, well hidden from view. Finally, Sally gave up and sat down.

"What's wrong? Is Jack okay?" I asked and she burst into tears. I touched her lightly on the shoulder, but she cried even harder. I patted her and gave her a tissue I carried around to wipe up Lambert's drool after a hard walk. She dabbed at her eyes and then straightened up to say something.

"He has to stay overnight for tests." She sobbed and then began to cry louder. Jack remained underneath Lambert. I could see his point of view. I could even understand why his person would be upset. The idea of being separated from Lambert would send me straight to my bed. I again began to wonder if Lambert and I lived in a codependent relationship.

"What's wrong with him?" I asked and immediately realized how idiotic this question must sound to a distraught mother who had no clue herself.

"His stomach is swollen, he belches constantly and has terrible gas, and today they found some blood in his stool."

"Oh, but that could be anything." I said. "Can't they give a dog a colonoscopy?"

"I think that's what they have in mind, but he's such a sensitive little dog, they didn't want to mention it in front of him. I think they are looking for cancer." Sally whispered the last word so Jack couldn't hear, but Lambert heard and swung his head around to glance at me and then frowned. I could tell he felt aggravated by the whole ordeal. I did, too, for that matter. I hadn't a clue what Sally expected of me. As a new dog owner, I had no experience with the complexity of people's relationship with their dogs and didn't feel confident enough to say one night apart wouldn't hurt either one of them. Just then a technician came bustling over wearing gloves and a white lab coat.

"Come here little fella," he said to the invisible Jack while holding out his arms fully expecting him to be cooperative. Lambert had himself so neatly wrapped around his friend that you couldn't even see his curled tail. "Well, where is he, Mrs. Johnson?" The technician bent down to take a look under all the chairs. Lambert began to growl, a low intense growl punctuated by a few snarls. The technician swirled around and eyed him suspiciously. Lambert growled louder. Another technician appeared and the two of them stared at Lambert not knowing exactly what to do. Whimpering sounds came from under him accompanied by Sally's continued sobbing. I really didn't like other people's drama and had little patience for my own, so I mentally removed myself from the unpleasantness and watched as the two technicians reached under Lambert to drag out the frightened little dog.

Lambert went into overdrive and lunged at them with his lips pulled over his teeth. His behavior shocked me. I only knew Lambert as a sweet and loving friend. I had no clue as to why he felt so protective of the little dog. Just then Maggie appeared with a syringe. "I told you to have him neutered, Heddy. He would be a lot more docile." I suddenly realized she meant to give Lambert a shot of something, probably a tranquilizer. I thought it was intended to calm Jack's nerves. Just as she bent down to stick Lambert with the needle, I shoved away her arm and grabbed Lambert by his leash and hurried both of us out the door. Lambert barked over his shoulder at Maggie just before the door banged behind us. He leaned against me on the small porch and cried. I could see tears fall from his eyes and disappear into his fur.

"Come on, boy. You know I won't let anyone hurt you. I'm sorry about your friend. I'll call his mom tomorrow and find out what's wrong with him." I remembered the technician called her Mrs. Johnson. I made a mental note to find Sally Johnson and inquire about Jack's health tomorrow. I then realized dogs and children must bring their friends' parents into our lives whether we wanted them there or not. I sighed and used a Kleenex to mop up Lambert's tears.

We sat in the car for a few minutes to pull ourselves together after the waiting room ordeal. I talked to Lambert about Daniel. "I know you liked Daniel. I did, too, and if he were in our lives right now, we could call him on speaker phone and talk to him about the ordeal we both just suffered. To think that arrogant professor who doesn't even know a thing about me, expects me to call his secretary. I didn't even know the term secretary was still used. It's denigrating to women. The more sympathetic boss calls his assistant just that – an assistant. Can you imagine what life would be like living with a man who has a secretary and hits on women in the vet's waiting room? I mean, Lambert, he could be married for all we know and what do you think he does to arrive at his scientific conclusions on dog behaviors? How many dogs has he made miserable by watching them like lab rats? Oh Gawd, Lambert, it's too much to think about. My nerves are shot.

Let's go see Johns. He's the closest thing I have to a male friend."

I wiped up some more tears from Lambert's eyes and snuggled against the side of his neck. How did I exist without this sweet being in my life? Tears began to roll down my cheeks over the thought of being without Lambert, even for a night like Jack's poor mom had to suffer. I thought about the fun he had on Daniel's farm and wondered why he was more adaptable than I was when being in a new environment. I wondered why Lambert threw the decorator pillows off the bed before I had a chance to turn down the covers. I wondered about a lot of things, but mostly I wondered what I would do without the love of Lambert.

I pulled myself together and drove away from the animal clinic just as that horrid bespectacled man came running after my car waving another business card in the air. He must have found the one I threw in the trash and thought it was a mistake on my part. I reached for the cell to call Daniel, but quickly realized I didn't have his number. I would have to look him up on the computer later and Google his name.

I could see Johns hurrying past the hair dryers when he heard us knocking on the salon doors. "Hey doll, what's the ruckus about?" Johns stood back to let us by and then relocked the doors. "You both look a little disheveled. Let me give you a spritz and a quick blow dry. What's wrong with my favorite doggie client?" Johns bent over to scratch Lambert behind the ears and when noticing little response, further grilled me on our latest comings and goings. I spent entirely too much time telling him about my new Capri pants and the horrid professor when really Jack's and Sally's experience affected me more.

"Well, doll, I can see why being hit on by a Harvard professor would be distressing. I mean they are as dry as toast. I know. I had one or two of them myself. Even, Charo slept through the whole thing. It was that uneventful."

Then I told him about Jack and his mom. Lambert listened attentively and Johns, I noticed, behaved more sympathetically toward Lambert than me. "Oh, you poor dear; Jack's your little friend, and they were trying to hurt him."

I swear I saw Lambert nod his head in agreement. I just couldn't believe Johns had managed to get at the reason for our discombobulated state so quickly, but then he does have a dog although not much of one compared to Lambert. I mean how much affection can a person get from something that only weighs five pounds and has to take a pill every morning to keep her nerves calm?

"Let me give you both one of Charo's pills. They work wonders. I take them myself when my clients want to look like Miley Cyrus."

Lambert made himself comfortable in one of the salon chairs and even pushed it around so he could see both of us while we sat and talked about our day. I stuck Charo's nerve pills in my pocket and told Johns about our original reason for visiting Maggie. He suggested I buy Dr. Pitcarin's book *Complete Guide to Natural Health for Dogs and Cats.*

"Charo, poor little thing, had one of those, and I thumbed through Dr. Pitcairin's book, which I call my bible vet, and found a recipe for skin problems. Boil water and throw a sliced lemon in the boiled water and let it sit overnight. Apply it to the affected area twice a day and voilà, my dear, gone, just like that. No nasty vet bills or messing about with creams and salves."

"Thanks, Johns. We'll try that." I heard myself say 'we' again. Now, Lambert and I have become a couple. I refer to every activity as something we do together: we visited with Johns, we went painting, we ate dinner on the porch and we went to bed. I wondered if this were normal pet lover behavior, and if I would settle so comfortably into my new relationship that I wouldn't even need to go prowling about the countryside looking for a man who satisfied both Lambert and me.

"Is it normal to refer to your pets as we?" I asked Johns while he busied about trying to reconstruct my hair.

"Oh, doll, everything's normal in the pet world. Just don't ever tell a non-dog lover anything Lambert does that you think is adorably cute. They look at you like you have a screw loose. But tell a dog lover and soon you'll be swapping stories about all your dear pets and become the best of friends in the dog park. You'll love these people in context but probably won't want to take them home with you. I made that mistake with Charo. The first man with a poodle who fawned over my Charo, I let in my house and he didn't leave for two weeks. Seems he and the little pouf ball were between living quarters and well, I was just such a softy with my little Charo puppy. My new border found a rich man with two Dobermans who have probably battered the little pouf by now. I mean the dog not his owner. Oh my, I am funny today." Johns laughed heartily allowing me the extra minute to get the pouf double entendre, and then I laughed too loud for Lambert. He gave out a sigh of resignation and eyed us both with suspicion.

Later Lambert and I went for a walk around the neighborhood. We enjoyed being together and even I took a sniff of nature along with Lambert who stuck his nose in every flowering bush we passed and then stopped a moment to enjoy the fresh smell of goat manure one of our neighbors used for fertilizer. I had to hold my breath to keep from taking in the smell, but Lambert all but burst into song over the fecund odor. Occasionally, he nuzzled my leg and glanced up at me with a smile on his face. I remembered what Johns said about it being all right to tell other dog lovers about every adorably cute thing your dog did each day. I wished I had someone to regale stories of Lambert's brilliance, but only Mr. Dodder came to mind and maybe Karma but she already seemed to know.

Jack's mom also came to mind as a willing listener to Lambert's escapades. Pre Lambert I would have dismissed Sally as a silly woman in love with her dog, but now all I felt was compassion. I even gave some thought to including Lambert in my paintings, but I had never painted an animal before falling in love with one myself. I began to wonder about the human heart. I began to understand the heart chooses the one we love. I caught myself sounding philosophically simple and shoved these thoughts aside and joined Lambert who was busy sniffing a rambling rose hanging over someone's white picket fence.

Just then I heard someone calling my name. "Heddy! Heddy!" I looked around but didn't see anyone. Lambert jerked at his leash and caused me to lose my grip. He shot off in the direction of our house. I ran after him. Fortunately, I had changed into my comfortable cross trainers and wasn't still encased in the fancy designer products Karma insisted I wear to attract a man. Yet, I could hear one calling my name and for a moment I felt a surge of excitement. Lambert kept looking back to make sure I was behind him, until finally, he stopped and grabbed ahold of my hand and pulled me up our driveway to be presented to Daniel. Lambert all but jumped into his arms while I stood perplexed over my own feelings of happiness. I couldn't believe the enthusiasm I felt at seeing the same man I had verbally lambasted for being a misogynist, and now he appeared to be warm hearted and handsome and worthy of my attention. I could feel myself move toward him.

"Hope you don't mind. Since you didn't get to finish your chili the other day, I made a fresh batch and brought you and Lambert some." Lambert stood with his nose buried in Daniel's crotch, but he didn't seem to notice. I felt a twinge of embarrassment at my dog's behavior and then quickly thought maybe this was some kind of male bonding ritual. I realized I knew very little about the male animal of any species. I knew they were important for procreation but was confounded over why female humans seemed to make such a fuss at having one enclosed in the same living space with them. I made a mental note to ask Karma.

Before I could thank Daniel for his thoughtfulness, a familiar back-fence voice intruded upon our privacy. "Heddy, what's this? First yuh get yuhself a dog and now yuh bringing home a man. Gunna keep him, too?" Mr. Dodder asked.

"Mr. Dodder, this is Lambert's friend Daniel." I turned red from embarrassment. I don't know what possessed me to refer to Daniel as Lambert's friend. I could feel my face flush, and I all but burst into tears and shut myself in the house, but

Lambert let go of a joyous bark and grabbed my hand in his mouth and stuck it in Daniel's free hand, the one not sheepishly holding onto a crock pot full of soup.

"Bin telling Heddy here, dog needs a real job. No regular fussy lap dog she got. Real working dog. Yuh from around these parts?"

Daniel's face lit up with an amused half smile over Mr. Dodder's inquisition, but he acted as though it was an everyday exchange in his life. "Yes, I live out on Farm Road One and, yes, I agree Lambert does need a job, but I also think he's fortunate to be taken in by someone who is so devoted to him."

"Don't believe in making a sissy outta a real workin' dog," Mr. Dodder replied and Lambert ran over to the fence and jumped up to bark in Mr. Dodder's face. "Well, Heddy, think he's a good 'un. Guess yuh better off keeping both of um." Then to my relief he plodded off to tinker with something.

"I'm so sorry about that," I said, still feeling flustered over the entire exchange.

"Oh, don't be. He's right of course."

"About what?"

"We're both 'good 'uns!" He laughed, and I laughed. Lambert wagged his tail and then began nudging both of us toward the back door until we were all three standing in the kitchen.

I placed three bowls on the table and reheated the chili for supper. We ate together like a family. I no longer felt guarded against Daniel's intentions, maybe because there was a ring of truth in my neighbor's words about Daniel being the one worth keeping in my life.

6

Lambert Weighs In:

Kiss my hairy butt if it hasn't been a roller coaster ride of emotions with Mom and her never-ending problems communicating with the male of her species. I had settled myself nicely into HH's world of hair balls and an indoor jungle of plants that would rival any botanical garden, when all of a sudden, I'm being yanked out the door and back down the path I had just run up. I could hear the poor bastard calling after Mom wanting to start over and who could blame him. I was beginning to feel sorry for any man who engaged in conversation with her. A man's words seemed to trip her emotional landmines leaving an array of body parts trailing along behind her while she high tailed it back home to her safety zone. Needless to say, my disappointment hung heavy in our car during the ride home and to make matters worse the old codger next door has not stopped carping about Mom getting me a proper job.

My loyalty, of course, would always be to the one who saved me from Idiot Farmer's clutches and a harrowing life of sheep and dirt. If it hadn't been for Mom, my nose would have found itself permanently stuck up a sheep's butt. I love my nose and use it to smell all the wondrous odors around our house. Even the old codger's whittling next door gave off a faint smell of fresh wood, not to mention, his cherry smoking tobacco stuffed inside a pipe that he had carved from the limb of a walnut tree. Nope. I loved Mom best no matter whether or not she followed my plans for bettering our lives. Actually, I came to realize Mom didn't know I had plans, and so any hopes I had of merging our lives with HH and his hair balls would have to be curtailed till another opportunity presented itself. I thought about finding my way back to his house but didn't have the heart to leave Mom alone. She spent at least two hours dampening my fur with her tears. I can't tell you the effect this had on my nerves. I could practically hear them begging me to do something about the human person spilling her sadness onto their sensitive doodad wiring.

I just wanted to go sit in a corner and tidy up my balls. Somehow this activity, though odious sounding, gave solace to my nerves. Once out of sheer curiosity, I clicked onto the dog grapevine and asked my compatriots if they felt the same way. The grapevine practically short-circuited from all their unanimous responses. They couldn't just agree but felt the need to go into every private detail on methods used for various and inventive ways of accomplishing this task. Even Jack tossed in his two cents worth though being sans balls, no one took him seriously, so he had to pipe down and listen enviously to triumphant stories of cleanliness.

Mom stopped crying the second she noticed something amiss among all the fur on my back. I really didn't need more hysteria piled upon the original reason for her caterwauling. Next thing I knew, she's on the phone to Maggie the Butcher and an hour later, I find myself sitting in the vet waiting room staring at Jack's sad face.

"Hey buddy, why the long face?" In Jack's case a long face would be a euphemism for sad what with his flattened snout causing his face to turn round as a pie pan. Poor guy mumbled something about his mother now squeezing orange juice to add to his culinary breakfast feast further aggravating his stomach and causing him to shit blood. I commiserated with him for a while and tried offering suggestions like the most obvious - stop eating his mom's cooking until she gets the message. He didn't want to hurt her feelings. Said she smiled all the time she cooked and talked about what a 'sweet little man' he was and how much mommy loved him. The whole thing nauseated me. If Mom talked to me like I was a three year old human toddler, I would be forced to show her some of my exceptional Border Collie moves and get rid of any notion I would respond to bullshit, baby talk speech patterns of googoo gaga. Nope. I had my dignity to uphold, but poor Jack looked done in and defeated by his good heart and a weak stomach.

I wanted to tell Jack to act like he's got some balls, and then I remembered he didn't have them anymore and maybe this was part of his problem. I wondered if human males had to endure the eternal discussion of neutering every time they went to visit their own doctor for some simple procedure like having a wart removed or getting a chest X-ray. Judging by the constant adjusting that takes place every time I see one of them sitting for any extended period of time, I would guess they managed to hang on to theirs but didn't know quite where to put their animal zoo to keep from squashing it while sitting. The man in the waiting room squirmed all over his seat. He stared excessively at Mom, which annoyed me. I would have to discourage any thought he might be entertaining about taking Mom home with him. Not that I had to worry much, because as Karma said, Mom was batting zero in the man department.

My attention returned to Jack sitting on his mom's lap. This alone annoyed me. Why couldn't he sit on the chair next to her like a real dog? I mean, he could be giving the rest of us a bad rep by this dependent display on his human person. "Hey, buddy, buck up. Maybe there's a pill to ease the farts." Jack didn't take heart in this prospect. He had already gone too far down in his own misery to be pulled back up. I wanted to join him in the exam room but was afraid of Maggie the Butcher. Guess I had my own fears. I also wanted to tell Mom she wasn't a good judge of people. This, of course, became obvious when she leaped the fence at HH's house in her hurry to get away from a perfectly good male. She thought Maggie the Butcher was the cat's meow of vets when in fact the knife wielding vet delighted in deballing every male who walked in the door on four legs. I allowed my mind to wonder for a few seconds over whether or not she had had a go at her own husband. I could hear myself laugh over the image of his running for safety. Seconds later, Jack walked slowly through the exam room door and glanced back at me with the most forlorn expression I had ever seen since my siblings and I had been thrown in a bucket of milk.

The man in the waiting room eyeballing Mom struck me as bad news. The hair ball goofing off next to him was a different story. Boy, did she have a mouth on her. Kept calling her human Dad a real shithead, and said she thought I was a handsome devil for a dog and did I want to nuzzle her fur. Naturally, not wanting to hurt the fur ball's feelings by rejecting the offer, I made my way over and gave a quick sniff but couldn't resist expressing my unhappiness at the pair of eyeballs, so I shoved my nose in his ear and gave him a piece of my mind. Don't think he got the message, just kept staring at Mom. I could smell her sweat and knew she was worrying over something unpleasant. Figured it was him. My insides began rumbling but I knew better than to choose that time to fowl up the air with my disgruntlement.

Soon Jack came bounding out of the exam room and rammed himself against my under carriage. Hysterical little guy kept screaming something about them wanting to keep him for good. I guess he changed his mind about all the missed opportunities on account of his neutered status, and now all he wanted was the safety of his own home. He kept squawking about Maggie the Butcher wanting to put a hose up his butt to take a look at him from the inside. His mom sat useless on her chair while my own Mom patted her shoulder. The dog drama going on in the waiting room played out like a reality show when the lab coat appeared and began looking under all the chairs for Jack. I could feel him shaking against me and held him tighter while trying to figure out how to hurry us to the nearest exit. Not being as dumb as he looked, the lab coat spotted Jack's tail sticking from under my fur. Naturally, I bared my teeth and growled full throttle hoping to scare the pinhead into backing off, but the next thing I knew Maggie the Butcher was careening around the corner holding a syringe as big as a turkey baster. Fortunately, Jack couldn't see the malevolent expression on her face when reaching to sink that thing in my butt. Mom grabbed me just in time and pulled me outside.

I'm embarrassed to say I just sat down and cried like a sniffling chipmunk over Jack's fate at the hands of Maggie the Butcher. Mom kept wiping up my tears and telling me she would check on him. But I had doubts about leaving my best friend to fend for himself and suffer the indignity of laying down for a crazy vet with a diploma giving her the right to do anything she wanted to a helpless animal. Life sure seemed unfair at that moment, and then I realized for every good person like Mom and HH, there were other human persons who had a little bit of bad in them. This thought sobered me fast and I walked close to Mom's new pants, sniffing the fresh smell of starch and laundry detergent. I still preferred the bags she used to wear, but knew any preference for Mom's clothes paled in the face of Jack's plight, so I shoved the thought aside and jumped in the passenger seat next to Mom. We sat for a while stuck in sadness and worry. My nerves had taken a beating lately and well, I could tell by the smell Mom's had gone into overdrive dealing with her scattered emotions. She mentioned how nice it would be to talk to Daniel and well, of course, I entertained that very thought but said nothing. My insides still rumbled from the stress of it all, but what with both Maggie the Butcher and the old codger so far up my hairy butt, I didn't think there was room enough to let go of a good fart.

Mom drove us to her friend Johns who was nancying about his empty salon enjoying the sounds of some crazy salsa music. I think Mom liked him because he made her laugh and she could be herself, and he's not going to tell her everything will be all right if she just takes a warm bath. I heard Karma say that to her once and then was surprised to see Mom turn red and yell something about a warm bath just wouldn't cut it. Well, from a dog's point of view a warm bath would only make any situation worse. No, Johns offered both of us Charo's nerve pills but Mom said no, maybe later. If I had been allowed to answer for myself, I would have taken the whole bottle.

While Mom poured out all her sad sack stories, I got busy tuning into the dog grapevine to try and contact Jack. I could hear him whimpering and when I asked, "What's up little guy?" he yelped a couple of times and then went back to whimpering. I sensed he had been put in some dark place behind bars. Jack certainly wasn't his loquacious self, probably because he'd been subdued by the ordeal of being separated from his mom and nearly frightened to death by the lab coat. I tried again by giving him a good telepathic tongue lashing on worrying me to death. He shot back something about his insides having been cleaned out, and now he waited in a cage for Maggie the Butcher to take photographs. Here he got a little hysterical, because he said something about wondering why she would want a picture of his butt in her photo album. Jack needed a nerve pill, too. I could tell his nerves bristled from fright. Poor little guy.

While lounging about in one of Johns fancy chairs, I let my mind wonder to imagine where my heroic, older brother might be. I imagined him happy with a nice family living on a farmette like HH's but soon realized with all my machinations I couldn't get me and Mom out on the farmette to enjoy the best of nature so what chance did a Border Collie worthy of its name have in relocating to an idyllic lifestyle. No, my heroic, older brother demonstrated resourcefulness and courage the day he saved my new born self from drowning in a pail of milk. Idiot Farmer would want him for a real working dog or sell him to the highest bidder. My daydreams stalled out the moment I realized he could be anywhere. If I ever got the gumption to get off my hairy butt and go find him, at least I still had the smell of him tucked in my brain.

Johns and Mom did their usual air kissing good byes when done cavorting with the language of woe. We drove home and immediately set stride for a walk. I could smell the old codger coming toward us behind his fence but we were down the driveway before his head appeared over the top to say something about my lay about lifestyle. I laughed to myself and then joined Mom's stride and began enjoying the smell of flowers and goat manure. Nothing made my nose happier than a good sniff of something ripe. Cooking smells coming from all the houses wrapped their aromas around my nose and sent me to swooning like a Dodo bird at the feet of a Peacock.

I could feel Mom's anxiety slip away as we walked around the neighborhood together. She even laughed when a bee made itself at home on the end of my nose. I didn't think it was so funny and nearly went cross eyed looking at the ugly thing. Finally, Mom blew the bugger off to land on a nearby flower where it belonged. I don't need a botanical lesson to understand the important role a bee plays in keeping our gardens lush. Nope. I just didn't want to be caught up in the process and have some testy Yellow Jacket hammering my nose for emotional relief. Dogs are bound to cross paths with them because we have a tendency to lead with our noses. Sometimes, I forget there's a body attached to my nose when on the scent of a particularly fecund smell that beckons me to follow it to the source. I call it the hunt. I try to curtail this enthusiasm for the times when Mom is not attached to the other end of my leash to slow me down.

We sauntered along the sidewalk happily enjoying each other's company when all of a sudden a familiar smell hit my proboscis like a head on collision. I could smell HH standing nearby with his homemade chili. Since Mom's nose had a short snout, I figured HH wasn't registering with her limited olfactory abilities and it was up to me to hurry us along before he lost interest and drove away in his tiny pickup truck. Being a vegetarian he had an entirely different smell from all the meat eaters happy to take a bite out of anything that moves. He smelled fresh, like a straight from the garden odorous mixture of wheat grass and barley joined by the sweet smell of pineapple. I knew Mom could do worse and probably would if left to sort through her mental wrangling on whether or not she could stomach having a male in her life other than Yours Truly, of course. She enjoyed the reservoir of love I had to offer but had doubts about a male human hanging in there for the long run like a devoted dog.

We rounded the bend and hurried up the driveway to where HH stood grinning with uncertainty and fear, probably of Mom calling the police to have him brought up on stalking charges. Nope, this wasn't going to happen. Mom let loose of all her previous doubts the second she laid eyes on the man who had the wherewithal to arrive unannounced and carrying a gift he had made himself. Mom being stunted in the social department didn't help much, but still she smiled and invited him inside. Then the old codger trudged out of nowhere and got involved by carping to HH about what a lazy waste of space I turned out to be and how Mom just didn't grasp the concept of locking me to a chain gang somewhere in the deep south where a man earned the dollar he made every day and thanked the mosquitoes for keeping him awake.

None of his gibberish made sense to HH and so he just smiled and agreed with Mom's dog rearing methods. You'd have thought I hadn't suffered enough when arriving in the school of hard knocks straight from my own mother's womb. I learned a thing or two early on about not succumbing to the expectations of others. If I had, Idiot Farmer would be arranging my daily calendar to suit his redneck idea of how a dog should be utilized to serve man. I had also seen how he treated his coon dogs to keep their noses in tip top shape. They suffered a diet of raw meat, life in an outdoor pen with the occasional opportunity to chase a raccoon up a tree so Idiot Farmer could shoot it for fur. The shot gun blasts alone nearly made them all deaf, not to mention, their having to suffer from the ordeal of running in front of an idiot carrying a loaded gun off safety. Nope, I learned early on that life could be a whole lot better than what most of us are born into. We just got to step off the grid.

I moved HH and Mom away from all the honking noise coming from the old codger by using a sideways herding technique, which often comes in handy when keeping humans within eyesight of where I want them to be. HH had caught on to my management style early in our acquaintance but said little to alert Mom. He didn't mind being mano-a-mano with a dog, which elevated him to Border Collie status in my book. I didn't think Mom could do better than having HH as her human mate, especially not with all her social shortcomings. I mean, yesterday, I heard her tell one of our neighbors that she thought the giant urn in her front yard looked like a man's penis. The neighbor's face turned into a crumpled hood ornament and she began to cry. Mom didn't know what to do with her tears, so she blundered on by telling her there was nothing wrong with a man's penis so long as it was kept in his pocket. I thought about walking on ahead and pretending I didn't belong to the strange woman on the other end of my leash but didn't want to desert her for mismanagement of words. I loved Mom and only wanted what was best for her.

They spent the evening on the couch, mostly talking, but occasionally I noticed HH would reach over and touch Mom's hair like he had some sort of fascination with the few wispy strands of fur she had growing on her head. I figured I could interest HH into massaging my whole body if I shoved myself next to his other hand that wasn't doing much except dangling off the couch. I strategically arranged my body so his hand lay on my right shoulder, which was certainly in need of a thorough going over what with all the stress I had to endure lately. His hand laid there for a while until finally I moved back and forth, and he caught onto the idea he was supposed to get busy and relieve the tension suffered by this hard done by dog.

Once HH put his mind to something, he did a thorough job of it. He went at my body like an experienced masseur working at a five star porn resort. I nearly peed myself from happiness; it felt that good. A few minutes later, I dragged my limp body to rest on our bed after first throwing off the extra pillows and pulling back the bed covers. Wouldn't you know, the second my head hit the pillow, Jack got on the dog grapevine and announced he had just had a tiny camera stuck up his butt and been photographed from one end to other. Naturally, I asked what was on the photographs. Jack seemed fuzzy on the details but said something about his insides looked like they had been doused with jalapeño pepper spray.

"Hey little guy, no shit surprise from what you been eating. Maybe now you'll learn to say no. Gotta be tough, little guy. They give you anything for the pain?" I asked but heard nothing. Again I gave him a telepathic tongue lashing for upsetting the feel good mood I had been enjoying previous to his bleating into my ear. He rallied enough to mention a large dose of Pepto-Bismol. I laid my worries to rest for the night, knowing my best friend would probably be back home tomorrow.

Eventually, HH disappeared into the night and Mom bounded upstairs to our bedroom and asked me if I needed to go outside. I could practically hear myself snore so she left me alone and began the ritual of getting herself ready for bed when suddenly I noticed she was singing, not quite as melodic as a bird but a happy, feel good sound that made me smile and imagine us all together on HH's farmette.

7

Here I was nearly forty years old and absolutely giddy over a man. I never thought in my wildest dreams I would find a man that would turn my attention away from art long enough to appreciate the good feeling that comes when he wraps his arms around my body. I had always considered men to be a distraction from a hard day's work, but Daniel seemed to flow in and out of my life without being a nuisance and, in fact, his presence had a calming effect that allowed me to go through my day without the usual low lying worry of wondering if there's something missing. This new feeling let me focus unencumbered by extraneous emotion on the business of art.

The canvases for my one woman show fell due in two weeks; I needed one more painting to cover the walls. I had run dry of ideas and was in need of inspiration. Just at that moment, Lambert walked up and shoved his nose against mine so our eyes met in some quixotic dog way. While nose to nose with my dog, it occurred to me Lambert would make a good subject. I had never painted a dog or wasn't given to go all romantic over the idea of slapping faces on my bare canvases and then swooning over the beauty to be found in the human countenance. However, getting a close up view of Lambert's limpid brown eyes and the straight line of his nose ending in a damp shade of black might just be the inspiration I needed to cull the artistry of my inner recesses to discover what's there if anything.

"Lambert, would you like to hang in a gallery for people to see how truly handsome you are?" I asked and then waited for a response. He barked a couple of times and wagged his tail, which I interpreted as an enthusiastic yes. We set to work creating a backdrop for him to pose against. I had some fussy silk pink material I thought would counter balance his stocky masculine body, but he yanked it from the makeshift platform and then ran out of the room. He returned seconds later dragging in his plaid pillow and then shoved the thing against the wall and sat in front of it. He even tilted his head upright in some regal pose he must have thought befitting a well-bred Highland dog. "Okay, I can work with that. I can see you'll make a good model. Let's just hope you have the patience to sit for a period of time."

Three hours later, I had rendered several interesting likenesses of Lambert among the drawings strewn across the floor. He had held the pose until I told him to take a break while I studied them. He stood next to me and mused over each drawing until finally putting his paw on the one I, too, thought the most interesting of them all. I had no idea dogs could discern subtle differences in objects drawn on paper. I thought they would appear as flat surfaces in varying shades of gray. He seemed fixed on that particular rendering, so I propped it against another easel and set to work using it as the model for my underpainting. Meanwhile, Lambert resumed his pose, which at this point was not necessary, but he seemed to enjoy being a model. After another couple of hours, I decided it was time for our break.

"Want to walk around the neighborhood, Lambert?" He ran to the bedroom closet and grabbed my walking shoes and met me at the back door holding his leash in his mouth with my shoes neatly arranged so they pointed outside. Lambert nearly brought tears to my eyes every time he did what some people might consider a small act of thoughtfulness but it felt like someone special cared about me. I wondered for a moment if Daniel would be as kind.

Our feet hadn't gotten down the back porch stairs when I heard a familiar voice coming over the fence. His off hand, invasive remarks to Daniel and the implication I needed two males to help move my life along still stung and left me a little less sympathetic to his plight of being a lonely old man. I no longer gave a thought to having him frame my paintings. I just knew he would put himself in charge of other more personal aspects of my life. Maybe, Lambert had been right in his earlier assessment of Mr. Dodder when peeing on his shoes. The man might just be what he appeared, a thorn in our side.

"Say, Heddy, how yuh getting along with yuh new feller?" His head now appeared just above the fence. The thatch of grey hair had always stuck straight up, coarse and uncombed, at least since I had moved into my bungalow four years earlier. I noticed no one ever came to visit him, and he seemed to go about his day without the need for companionship. I wondered then why he would show the least amount of uninvited interest in mine and Lambert's lives.

"Just fine, Mr. Dodder. Thanks for asking," I said and tried to hurry along but his fence gate opened before I had a chance to close mine. He studied Lambert with the same critical expression as a judge at the Westminster dog show.

"Got a different look about him. Yup. Satisfied with himself look. Yuh must have gotten him a job." Mr. Dodder leaned back on his heels and beamed.

"Yes, as a matter a fact, Lambert's been modeling for me. You were right, Mr. Dodder, when you said he needed a job. Nothing's more taxing than being an artist's model." I smiled, thinking finally the old man would give a favorable report on Lambert's new job.

"Well, yuh don't say. Not what I had in mind but yuh dog does seem a might impressed with himself like a real working sheep dog." Just as he finished expressing this last observation, a car veered into the driveway and came to a sudden stop not five feet from where we were standing.

"Hi there. Hope you don't mind. Maggie gave me your address. Just had to come and tell you the good news." Jack's mom began talking before her feet hit the pavement. Jack bounded out of the car and over to Lambert. "The results of Jack's colonoscopy show a nasty inflammation but no cancer, polyps or tumors. Maggie put him on a mild diet until all his linings heal and he gets back to normal."

"That's great news. I was going to call you but didn't have your number. Never occurred to me to ask Maggie," I said, mildly agitated at having my address given out by Lambert's doctor.

"Yuh don't say. Didn't know they gave dogs colonoscopies." Mr. Dodder piped in. I introduced them.

"Oh yes. They use all the latest technologies to take care of our animals." Sally smiled. Just then I noticed she had similar, only styled, gray hair as my neighbor's and seemed about the same age but considerably more charming with no lack of social skills.

I listened to the two of them go over the details of Jack's malaise with Mr. Dodder finally saying, "I always believe a dog should be treated like a dog and not be spoiled with table scraps. Don't have the same plumbing as people do."

"Oh, yes. You're very wise, Mr. Dodder." Sally responded with a pretty smile.

"Call me Sam."

I saw Lambert's ears move forward and could swear an expression of alarm flitted across his face, which was being licked excessively by Jack. Even I wondered at the familiarity between the two people who had moved themselves into my life and showed no signs of leaving. My years spent as a misanthrope had at this very moment come to an end causing me a slight twinge of nervous doubt. Just then, Lambert reached up with his right paw and slipped it into my hand. We stood that way for at least five minutes while watching the animated exchange taking place right in our own back yard. I simply did not know whether to be nauseated or elated, so I decided it would be best to let nature take its course.

We excused ourselves and again set about our neighborhood walk. Jack followed along happily, moving his legs like pistons to keep up with Lambert. When Lambert stopped to take in an interesting smell, Jack stood next to him and inhaled noisily through the tiniest nose holes I had ever seen on a dog. It seemed clear the little dog idolized Lambert. He kept glancing at him with an expectant look on his face. Periodically, Lambert would lean over and nudge the side of his face, causing his friend to collapse in happiness and emit tiny snorts that made me laugh. If my dog could take on the friendship of this needy little guy, then I could extend my good nature far enough to embrace all the new people edging themselves into my solitary world.

We returned thirty minutes later to find Sally admiring Mr. Dodder's hand-carved bird collection. I peered over the fence at the sight of him handing her an especially beautiful duck stained in different shades of blues and browns to show off its feathers. Sally handled the duck with such care you'd have thought it came from the Whitney Museum. The old man beamed with pride. I quietly opened the gate while Lambert gave his friend a gentle nudge indicating for him to rejoin his mom. She turned and waved but made no motion to come in our direction, so I quickly closed the gate and hurried back inside the house. Lambert and I sat and stared at each other, pondering the new turn of events. He rested his chin on my knee while I clutched a cup of coffee, wondering what was really happening on the other side of the fence. Lambert's sigh possessed the sound of resignation. Perhaps, I should do the same.

"Ready to get back to work?" I asked Lambert. Seconds later, he assumed his pose and let me spend the rest of the day studying perspective. The plaid background needed toning down, which I thought could be done by making it appear convex while Lambert himself appeared stalwart but with the tender feelings of compassion expressed in his brown eyes. True realism had never come off the end of my brush but rather a mixture of El Greco and Klee gilded with a sense of humor emerged on my canvas, always seeming to escape my real life perspective. Yes, I reflected for a moment, it was hard being me, mostly because I couldn't always find me except on a canvas and even those would often seem like they had been painted by someone else. I couldn't imagine why the art world had such a high opinion of my work. I never once took their tastes into consideration when dabbling with my paints. I gave very little thought to those who bought my paintings, or those who would want my paintings or even those who actually collected my paintings in hopes that I would die soon and drive up their value. No, my studio had always been a private world of solace even in my early life. My parents had never looked over my shoulder to comment on my Crayola drawings. They seemed to understand the sacred moments of my efforts to tap into a realm higher than the one where my body resided. My thoughts then plummeted to take in the meaning of my mother's death. She, too, hoped to go to a world lovelier than the one with nothing left in it but me. The day had suddenly turned sad, so I put down my brush and asked Lambert if he would like to go for a country drive.

We drove along the familiar roads in silence. Lambert stared out the window and I again rummaged through my own thoughts, hoping to permanently throw out a few and rearrange others in the furthest corners of my mind for future reference. Somehow my parents being physically beautiful people only made the loss of them more difficult. The door to beauty had been closed the day my mother died along with the daily peeks of a once vivacious woman. I remembered their laughter coming across the dining table where I sat with a box of colored pencils and drew imaginary people on large pieces of drawing paper. My imaginary people also laughed and rarely suffered a cloud in their made up horizons. Even their houses appeared happy and every blade of grass leaned into the sun. My drawings were cheerful reflections of a harmonious household until my father died and my mother began to waste away in despair. My imaginary people slowly disappeared from the drawing pages and instead hid themselves somewhere safe never to appear again.

I had told myself it was all a maturation process and had no psychological meanings beyond a simple putting away of what once was and is no more. The school guidance counselor insisted on adding dramatic meaning to the abrupt change of subject matter. She insinuated herself into my senior art class and annoyed my teacher with her psychobabble dissections of my required art assignments. My teacher went to the principal and asked to have her removed from my case but he refused and said it was in my best interest. The art teacher didn't agree and felt the greater need lay in giving my artistry the privacy to create what pressed itself to materialize on the end of my pencil. She then handed me two drawing pads. One full of happy faces she had drawn herself and the other one to be used only at night in the privacy of my room. After seeing a few of my teacher's drawings, the counsellor felt satisfied that I was on the road to recovering my mental health, and so she stopped appearing in class to coo over the happy faces. I suspected this bored her, and really she felt the most satisfaction when dealing with a semi schizophrenic teenager.

Lambert glanced over from time to time and smiled at me. I had come to accept his smiles as a personal display of satisfaction with our general compatibility. I smiled back at him and he returned to staring out the window. I had never made anyone happy before. I paused a moment to give that notion some thought. It troubled me and indicated an outward view toward the world and an expectation it existed to make me happy. It never once occurred to me that I might be able to put a smile on someone else's face. Perhaps, the psychobabble counsellor had a valid point in worrying about my mental wellbeing. I sounded selfish to myself. Yes, I appeared to be a selfish misanthrope with a jaundiced world view in constant need of critique.

I swerved the car around and headed in the opposite direction back to town. Fortunately, I had buckled Lambert into his harness. He remained unharmed by the sudden movement, but I could sense some confusion coming from the passenger seat.

"We're going to Karma's and picking out a couple of toys for Daniel's cats. I may need some help, Lambert. I have no idea what a cat would find amusing."

Karma greeted us like two long lost friends. Lambert had no patience for her gushing and went to check out the cat toys. I told her about seeing Daniel and trying to demonstrate some generosity by taking his cats a present. She complimented me on my savvy manipulation of a man's heart. I had no idea what she was talking about.

"Men love gifts. You'll have him eating out of your hand," Karma explained.

"That sounds disgusting and besides this is not a gift for him but his cats."

She laughed. I began to have doubts about expressing my feelings to someone else. I noticed she didn't wear a wedding ring, and realized I had never asked her if she had a husband.

"Are you married, Karma?"

"Oh yes, twenty-five years, now, to the loveliest of men. I give him gifts all the time. That's how I know, they like them. My George lights up when I take the time to sort through the Black & Decker electric tools at Home Depot to find something new for his workbench."

"Oh, that's very thoughtful of you." I mused over this revelation. I couldn't picture myself in the tool department of any store in search of the perfect gift for a man. But then, I had never been married and had no clue what a man would appreciate. The whole relationship thing had always been a puzzle to me. Once, I went out with a man who asked me to cook his supper after four dates. He appeared at my door step with a package of fresh fish and a box of rice pilaf. He said he liked his fish nice and crispy and his rice el dente. I told him I didn't have cooking oil to fry his fish nor a pan to fry it in. He told me there didn't seem to be any point in continuing our romance if I couldn't oblige him by making a home cooked meal once in a while. He even went on to give me the exact figures of the totaled restaurant meals.

"You need a crash course on how to please a man," Karma said.

"Oh, I don't think I want one. I'd rather bumble along and see what happens, see if he can manage all my eccentricities."

"Well, just don't forget you have to accept his eccentricities, also."

"You think he has some?" I asked, sounding alarmed.

"You're buying presents for his two cats. Obviously, he must have doted over them or you wouldn't think them important enough to bring gifts."

"Oh, you're right, but then I dote over Lambert, too." I remembered my latest observation when realizing I began referring to my dog and I as a couple.

"Yes, but that just makes it all very interesting. Now, let's see what Lambert has in mind for the little darlings."

We found Lambert surrounded by some tiny mice he had pulled from the racks. I apologized and tried to put them back. Karma found this amusing and bent over to laugh harder at the haphazard arrangement of stuffed mice running amuck in her store. Or so they appeared. Lambert sniffed each one of them. I had no idea why and must have looked puzzled.

Karma straightened and made an effort to contain her laughter. "He's sniffing for cat nip. Cats love it."

"What is it?"

"It's a special weed that makes them feel good."

"You mean like pot?" I asked and had an immediate vision of Daniel's cats lounging around the living room smoking from a bong.

"Well, something similar to pot only legal. Actually, now that you mention it, I had heard of heavy pot smokers running out of weed and dashing to the pet supply stores and buying up the cat nip. But that was back in the seventies. It's easy to grow."

"Maybe I should just take them a plant. What do you think, Karma?"

"I think we should let Lambert choose something for them. That would really make it special. They would be able to smell his drool on it." Karma smiled but I didn't quite trust her. I never thought cats had a high opinion of dogs and being territorial creatures, I couldn't imagine Daniel's cats getting excited over two tiny mice covered with Lambert's dog drool.

I studied the assortment on the floor and chose the little mice still in a protective covering. "What do you say, Lambert?" He barked and then went over to the stuffed animal display to sort through the colorful selection until coming upon one resembling himself. He brought it back and threw it at my feet and then sat down and stared at me. "What do you want, boy?" He pushed the stuffed dog closer until it was resting on my feet.

Then Karma chimed in, "Too funny, Lambert. You want the fluff balls to have a little Lambert. I can see it's slightly wet so the kitties will be able to smell you when you're not there." Karma seemed excited over this prospect, although I couldn't figure out why.

"Do you gift wrap?"

"Sure do." Karma led us to the backroom and searched for a box.

Minutes later we were on the road again and headed for Daniel's house.

8

Lambert Weighs In:

I sat for hours with my ear hung over the dog grapevine until finally learning Jack had been freed from the jail cell where Maggie the Butcher was holding him. Poor bastard whimpered all night and could hardly muster up a few words to let me know if there had been any permanent damage done to his sore butt. Eventually though, he went into excruciating detail over his ordeal. I could have used less information but knew the little guy had been traumatized at the reckless hands of the lab coat. The whole thing set my mind to ruminating over a dog's life. Human persons think nothing of working us to death, tossing us out the car window when we become a nuisance, or leaving us alone with a dog doctor whose medical scrutiny extends beyond her humanity. While caught up pondering the sorry plight of some dogs, I thought of my own good fortune in having a Mom who was convinced I'm a gift from the dog gods.

I decided to poke my nose in her studio and check on her state of mind. She and HH had slobbered all over each other on our couch the previous few nights and had now become a couple. This new development turned Mom into a dithering mess of smiles. She even lay in bed last night smiling while staring at the ceiling. I could hardly sleep from the brightness of her teeth glittering off the moonlight. It caused me a great deal of internal disturbance just knowing she lay there right next to me thinking about HH like he might be another gift suddenly appearing in her life without the helping paw of Yours Truly.

So when I saw her sitting in her studio looking as vacant as a shell left by a hermit crab, I wasn't surprised. I knew her mind had been crammed with visions of HH being the answer to a woman's prayers. I thought she needed a delicate reminder to get back to work. I shoved my nose hard against hers in an effort to tell her she need look no further than the end of her own nose to find abundance. That was how I ended up becoming a famous dog model. Can you just beat how a life can turn around on itself and come out better than it started? Certainly not Idiot Farmer who considered me a waste of space.

Mom and I created a perfect back drop to reflect my noble lineage. I know she had doubts I could sit long enough for her to draw a few strokes on a piece of paper but my rich inner life took over. I held my pose while engaging in various conversations on the dog grapevine. Did you know dogs were needlessly vaccinated and that only 5% of all rabies was caused by dogs? I also learned Martha Stewart put out a new line of fabric designs. I don't remember what female canine felt the need to share this tidbit of nonsense. I usually tuned into the professional watch dogs so I could keep up with the seamy side of a dog's life, catching drug dealers, crime solving murder cases, and sniffing after runaway convicts. Yep, it was definitely more interesting than those white collar detective stories Mom watched on the big box.

My friend Walter worked for the Boston Police department helping them with drug busts. His only complaint was not being called upon to make the official police statement to the press. He thought this must be an oversight by the department because he was their ace drug sniffer and highly respected by his human partners. I said, "Look, dude, you're a dog. Not like humans got the wherewithal to hear you. I mean, you got to accept they are limited when it comes to communication." This only made it worse. He started nattering on about being replaced by technology someday and probably ending up in a hospital sniffing for cancer cells. I reminded him the medical field was also a noble profession. But no, when Walter gets his shorts in a bunch, there's no talking to him so I decided to change the subject. I told him about wanting to find my heroic, older brother and he referred me to a German shepherd named Harry who worked in Missing Persons. I thanked him and stored the name in the back of my head for future reference.

The hours flew by with me holding the elegant pose of a noble dog while enjoying machine gun violence happening on the south side of our historic city. Mom had no clue her beloved companion visited the seamier side of life and enjoyed living vicariously through those who possessed considerably more courage, not to mention, earning power. Until that very moment, I had not given one thought to my bank account and wondered if Walter stuck his money under his mattress or invested it in gold, which in my mind appeared to be an unstable commodity but once again no one ever actually asked for my opinion. Except Mom, of course. She just asked me if I wanted to go for a neighborhood walk and my first thought was 'do bears shit in the woods'. I gathered up her walking shoes and hustled my hairy butt to the back door. If she would have let me, I could have hurried the process by putting her shoes on for her. Mom did draw the line when it came to familiarity. I didn't care if she watched me pee on the bushes but when it came to her own delicate emissions, she insisted I sit on the other side of the bathroom door. I kept telling her it would be faster if she peed outside along with me but once again my words just flew by her without landing anywhere near her ears.

The old codger, on the other hand, possessed the ears of a tree monkey and wouldn't you know it, he was front and center before Mom and I set foot on the driveway inquiring about my work life. I felt Mom's whole body go tense as a barn plank when seeing his squirrely face above the fence. I had to toe the line here and keep silent. Whoever said it was a free world had never been a dog. I've seen a dog wearing a muzzle for mouthing off at the wrong time so I bit my tongue, metaphorically speaking, and swallowed a nasty bark to prevent suffering the same fate by being strapped into something that looked like it could have been designed during the inquisition.

The old codger seemed perturbed at what he called my 'self-satisfaction'. Why shouldn't I be happy with myself, after all, I did display good judgment when it came to picking out a human person for myself? I mean, can you imagine if I had ended up at his house? I would be worked to death running errands for him, mowing the lawn, and probably cutting down the trees for the wood he used to make his silly ducks. I would have rather stayed tied to the vegetable stand and left on the side of the road than have that old codger as my lord and master.

Poor Mom, she stood there stiff as an ironing board until Jack's mom nearly ran us over with some old clunker she called a car. I could see smoke coming from her exhaust and had all I could do to keep from going into a coughing fit from the pollution hanging in our driveway. Jack flew out of the car like a trapped bat and slung his fat tongue on my face in an unseemly display of affection for two male dogs. I mean just because Jack had been neutered didn't make him gender-confused, but sometimes the little guy had boundary issues that required patience. I stood there and acted like I enjoyed having my face tidied up by someone else's tongue. After finishing the job, he began talking a mile a minute about his ordeal. I had already heard most of the stuff and sympathized greatly with his ordeal, especially about the part where he was strapped to a table and had his butt ransacked by Lab Coat's miniature camera complete with tripod. Jack kept quoting the 4th Amendment and how his rights had been violated along with his colon, which came under unreasonable 'search and seizure' as written up by our forefathers in the United States Constitution. I had to tell the little guy that our so called forefathers didn't have dogs in mind when whipping up the Bill of Rights and that these days most human persons were complaining about having their amendments violated and that he needed to keep up with the activities of the Humane Society if he wanted to know his own rights. I further pacified him by telling him it would be a good idea for him to talk to the animal communicator about his latest suffering and ask her to get word to the Humane Society. He liked this idea and I could tell he felt empowered by the way he strutted down the street with me and Mom on our walk.

Meanwhile, Mom had sunk into another low while watching Jack's mom and the old codger gabbing on about how best to treat a dog. This really tired my hairy butt. You'd think the old codger had an intelligent word to say on the subject but so far I hadn't heard him speak from a place of authority. I mean the old geezer didn't even own a dog that could give him feedback and just seemed to be one of those blowhards who had been living on God's green earth over half a century, which automatically made him an official spokesperson on every topic passing within hearing range. I have observed in my own short life that really intelligent human persons don't use others as sounding boards but instead wait to be asked for their position on a subject of interest to both parties. Mom had tired of listening to our blowhard neighbor a long time ago, so it boggled the imagination how he could be oblivious to her disinterest in his opinion. But I am only a dog and my purpose here was to comfort Mom not add fuel to the fire by getting up in the old codger's face about his own inadequacies.

I always loved a good walk, especially with amiable companions sniffing along with me. Jack stopped talking long enough to stick his nose in the flowers and take a hearty smell of the sweet mixture of jasmine and rosemary some well-meaning person had planted along the sidewalk, no doubt, for the enjoyment of others. Not sure the gardener had Jack and me in mind, but I was pleased to see Mom bend over and inhale the rhapsodic aromas. Watching Mom move along with a lighter step made me happy. I had put my hopes in HH delivering the goods when it came to treating Mom like the late blooming love goddess she wanted to be. I, of course, nauseated myself when making these observations, but I couldn't help getting caught up in their romance. It just seemed to spill over me and all of a sudden I envisioned myself standing at the altar with the preacher being wedded to the family of my choice. Life just didn't seem to get any better than having a family who both loved you like you were a being worth embracing in a circle of trust and entertained you with their zany sense of domestic life. I hoped we moved onto HH's farmette and not have to cram ourselves in the small house next to the old codger. In my mind, we all needed room to stretch out and claim our personal space so we could live in harmony. Then all of a sudden, it just hit me when I realized there might not be enough room in the big bed for HH and what if Mom and me managed to cram him in somewhere among the Martha Stewart designer bed coverings and once comfy, he began to snore. I can't abide night noises. Like most working dogs, I am a light sleeper causing me to jump up and go into protective mode when hearing any unusual sounds. HH's snoring would definitely fit into the category of unusual sounds. I realized it wasn't time for me to get my shorts in a bunch over something that may or may not happen. And now that I had given it thought, the two fur balls came to mind. I wondered if they expected to join us in bed or would they stay molded to the couch cushions. Life seemed full of unanswerable questions at that moment.

Jack startled me out of my reverie when peeing on the neighbor's sleeping Rottweiler. It boggles the mind to wonder why he didn't recognize the inert black object as being slightly dangerous; even trying to figure out why Jack wanted to put his scent on something that could snap him in two like a brittle twig was beyond comprehension. The aged watch dog stood at attention and reflected for a moment as though considering whether the canine pipsqueak was worth the effort it took to open his mouth and clamp his teeth around something soft. I snatched the opportunity to strut my telepathic powers of persuasion by agreeing with his moment of doubt when telling him the little guy suffered from brain damage and didn't recognize him as the mighty force sent to protect the less fortunate. He bought the ego trip lock, stock and barrel. He snorted and then went back to sleep. Jack, when realizing his error, tried to smooth over the whole mess by slapping his tongue on the soggy area he had just violated but this didn't go down very well, and I once again had to rescue him before his nemeses changed his mind and decided to take issue with Jack's momentary lapse of sanity.

We returned home in one piece and frankly I couldn't get rid of my best friend fast enough. I thanked him for stopping by and then shoved him through the old codger's gate back to his mom's loving arms.

Mom and I went back to work. I could feel the easy energy in her studio and even the sun shone through the skylight bringing in happy rays of light brightening our moods while enjoying the present moment. I sounded like a new age book when really dogs had it over humans by always living in the present moment except when worrying about the few cretins who didn't know it was in their best interest to treat us like their younger brothers and sisters. I mean, really, we're all living, breathing beings just trying to find a little peace. These cretins are the humans referred to earlier throwing their useless canines out the car window or dropping them along the side of the road to end up in shelters. They are a dog's worst nightmare. They suffered from the misconception of believing a dog exists without a soul.

This last thought prompted me to tune into my friend Fred who awaited adoption at one of the more enlightened animal shelters where they have a policy of not killing their guests for over staying their welcome. A small family of four came several times to study whether or not Fred would fit into their household. He lived in a constant state of anxiety worrying they would decide he wasn't a perfect fit and then move onto one of the more attractive dogs. Fred suffered terribly from an inferiority complex because of being a Beagle with a weight problem. He ate even more from the stress of not being wanted by this little family. He described the children as bipod angels with curly hair as dark as an American water spaniel. He said they smelled like peanut butter and ivory soap. I kept my ear hung over the dog grapevine and waited to hear what the little family had decided regarding Fred's fate. An hour later, I could hear him howling with glee when one of his caretakers told him his new family would be picking him up at five o'clock, and he would have to make himself look extra special nice by taking a bath and having a pedicure. At this point, Fred told me he wouldn't care if they polished his toes with hallelujah pink nail polish and doused him in Evening in Paris perfume to make him presentable to his new family. He was that happy. Another one of life's joyful endings always made me smile to myself.

I continued holding my pose watching Mom glance in my direction once in a while appearing pleased with her progress. She seemed the happiest when dabbing a brush in her paint pots and transferring the colors to the canvas where they got busy making something remarkable. Even I found her paintings a mysterious hint of realism gone awry to give the world a more humorous perspective. Yep, Mom had imagination. She didn't see things like exact replicas produced from a camera. She took ethereal acrobatic liberties with her surroundings when presenting them as not exactly what is being seen but rather what could possibly be there. I impressed myself with my own highbrow observations and wondered if I had missed my calling as an art critic, but then I quickly reminded myself dogs had a different set of options and that it was best if I didn't forget my early roots as being firmly established in the canine world. I also listed the benefits of being a dog as my affirmations when becoming frustrated over our dear human persons not understanding animals could communicate silently and thereby more effectively than our human counterparts. If they knew this, they would all be running to Jack's animal communicator to learn how to tap into that part of their brain that was lost during their own questionable evolution.

While I sat enjoying the country side from the passenger seat window, suddenly my head spun around with the car, and I found myself looking at the other side of the road going back the way we had just come. I wished Mom would give me some warning so I could brace myself to keep from getting whiplash. I had a hopeful moment we were traveling to spend a quiet evening at the farmette enjoying the sun dipping slowly into the ground while eating homemade soup. But minutes later, I found myself being given the dubious task of picking out toys for the two fur balls who would eventually be calling themselves my sisters. I knew they had a keen interest in small helpless animals, so I picked out a couple of mice stuffed with cat weed and a plush animal resembling Yours Truly for them to cuddle when they weren't high on weed and chasing after anything that moved.

Mom and Karma talked about love and other silly subjects while wrapping up the gifts. Occasionally, Mom would reach over and stroke me. I think she did this more to calm herself than to caress me with lighthearted tenderness. She leaned toward the nervous, uptight and not quite comfortable in her own body way of being. I noticed she was fraught with two ways of going about her day. While occupied with anything having to do with painting and her artwork, she moved about with the grace of a Pilobolus dancer but the times when required to be in the company of other people her body became jerky with anxious movements and a tendency to trip over a blade of grass growing away from the sun.

Mom sometimes reminded me of that blade of grass, not quite in sync with the world around her. I also noticed she seemed to become more and more comfortable with our walking together and even mindful of what was happening around her. The other day she cooed over a tree frog who for no good reason decided to leap on my back. I felt like tossing the ugly thing into the wind with one good shake but decided to stand still so Mom could lean over and take a good look at the bugged-eyed toad. I could feel him hopping from one end of my body to the other. He worked my last nerve by perching on my head; so needless to say, I lost complete control and flung him against the nearest tree. Mom bent down to make sure he had regained consciousness before continuing to move along with me. My attention had already wandered to the nearest bush, which I soaked with a good pee. I loved the outdoors in moderate doses and, as mentioned earlier, I preferred my fur to smell like the essence of me and not that of others, tree frogs included.

Once back in the car, we headed again in the direction of the farmette. I felt more confident we would actually end up there what with the trouble Mom had put me through in picking out a present for the two fur balls. When we drove up to HH's house, he stood outside staring at the large maple next to his driveway. He immediately left his thoughts somewhere when seeing Mom and me. He threw his arms around Mom and bent down to give me a nice scratch on the head. Actually, I much preferred to have my butt scratched but didn't think this was the time to bring up my own preferences. We needed to get Mom locked firmly in his heart before he felt like he couldn't live without Yours Truly.

Mom asked him why he had been staring at the tree. I couldn't believe his response.

"I was thinking about making Isabel and Philomena a tree house and then adding it to the Around the House series."

"Really? A treehouse for cats. How fortunate they are to have you looking after them."

"Well, they are family." He gave Mom a gentle hug and again patted the top of my head. I considered this last maneuver to indicate how much family met to HH and wouldn't it be nice if we were all one big happy family. I checked Mom for signs of stress. I couldn't smell any, but I knew she could bolt at any moment and take Yours Truly with her. I don't know why she viewed marriage to be a jail sentence; it's not as though humans mate for life like Turtle Doves and wolves. I mean even an Albatross mates for life, not to mention, some termites depending on whether or not the Queen takes a shine to one of the males and makes him her one and only King.

“What a lovely thought. I wonder if Lambert would like a treehouse. Imagine the stairs you would have to construct just so he could reach his doorway.” Mom began laughing, but I noticed HH had a serious expression on his face.

“What a novel idea. Do you really think Lambert would like a special place where he could view his surroundings? Keep an eye on things.”

Mom stopped laughing and stared at the object of her affection like he had lost his mind. “No, I was just kidding. Lambert’s afraid of heights and besides he prefers my bed over his, which indicates he likes his creature comforts.”

“I think he prefers to sleep with his mistress and who wouldn’t.” Mom swung her head around to stare at her beloved with a twinge of mistrust. I could smell the musky odor of anxiety. “What do you mean?”

“I mean you’re cuddly, soft and sweet. It’s a compliment.” He bent and kissed the top of her head. This had a calming effect on her. I wished he would do it more often.

“Oh, thank you.”

“Do you really think Lambert is afraid of heights?”

“Oh, yes. The other day I tried to get him to stand on top of the car so I could take a picture of him, and he wouldn’t have anything to do with it.” At this point HH was bent double laughing. Why would any self-respecting dog stand on the top of his Mom’s car? Imagine what the old codger would have to say about the sight of my stocky body looking like a hood ornament.

"My sweet, dear Heddy, a dog, especially one as smart as Lambert, weighs the importance of his dignity against the desire to please his much-loved human companion and decides his dignity has to remain intact for there to be mutual respect." Upon hearing this I again thought that this man was perfect for dragging to the altar. I could even hear myself sigh.

"Wow, I never thought of that. You're so smart when it comes to animals. But I still wouldn't spend a lot of time designing a staircase to a treehouse with the hopes of pleasing Lambert." They smiled at each other and walked into the house to give the two fur balls their present.

Mom sure nailed that right. I have always been a-four-paws-on-the-ground kind of dog. There was nothing ethereal about my world view that would find having my hairy butt hanging in the breeze an uplifting experience. I felt good about Mom understanding me and HH trying to please me. What more could a dog want?

The two furr balls lay right where we had left them after our last visit. Mom poked them with their present but didn't get a response. Dead as doorknobs, those two. I could not for the life of me understand why HH kept them around the house. You could see the hair fly off of them when they raised their heads to yawn. Once Mom and I take up residence at the farmette, they would be in for a shock. I've seen her with a vacuum cleaner and I quake at the memory of her trying to suck up the excess hair off my butt, which I have to admit does grow thicker in that area for no apparent reason. I nearly laughed out loud when just thinking about the comeuppance the fur balls would soon experience at the hands of a cleanup committee. Mom would probably bring that germ phobic foreigner from our house to dust off the furnishings and right now Isabel and Philomena appeared to be just that, furnishings.

Finally, Mom opened their present and waved the cat nip mice under their tiny noses. One sniff and they clamped their teeth around the heads of the mice and were off and running. Mom put the stuffed dog on the couch so they could cuddle it when returning for another nap. I watched them tear around the house, knocking a vase and two plant pots off their stands. HH didn't even blink an eye at their shenanigans and wouldn't let Mom clean up the mess. He told her to leave it that the plants needed to be repotted anyway. I could feel the anxiety drain from Mom's body. She must have thought he was going to hand her the broom and dust pan. Poor Mom. Even I knew she possessed little knowledge of what was expected of her when trying to interact with her own species. Her nerves spent their time in constant alert mode and only lay about doing nothing when she spent alone time with Yours Truly and fell happily into being herself. Eventually, I hoped she would come to realize HH possessed similar qualities to her beloved canine companion allowing her to give her nerves a rest in his easy going company.

HH opened the back door and he and Mom settled comfortably on a wooden swing suspended from the beams of the porch roof. I trotted across the field running in large circles until tired enough to lie on a grassy knoll and watch my new family go about the business of loving each other. Seconds later, the fur balls thought it would be great sport to hide their cat nip mice in my fur. My own nerves remained unruffled over the home invasion.

9

My romance with Daniel seemed to go at break neck speed. Sometimes I felt out of control of my own feelings and my behavior surprised me with its lustiness of a heroine in a romance novel. When lying next to him, I found myself purring from contentment. I had never experienced contentment except when holding a paint brush or studying the side of a barn as a possible subject to be put on canvas. I could stare at Daniel all day and never tire of his face, a handsome, rugged visage worthy of contemplation. I had forgotten about his unfortunate remarks during mine and Lambert's first visit. I even overlooked what I thought to be a peculiar fondness for his cats. Upon reconsidering this last thought, my love of Lambert could be considered excessive if someone cared to notice we have not been separated for more than an hour since his arrival in my life.

Mr. Dodder brought up the subject when saying Lambert needed to spend more time with his own species and less with the lady of the house, but I had begun to tire of Mr. Dodder's opinion and was now relieved to see him step out in the company of Jack's mom. I had no idea what she saw in him, but maybe we all wore blinders when it came to love. This brought me quickly back to the current examination of my romantic state of affairs. I worried I might miss something in Daniel's character, a malevolent undercurrent, a goatish disposition, or even a predilection for successful artists rather than just wanting the love of a good woman. No, I concluded, Lambert wouldn't be lobbying for him to become part of our family if Daniel possessed a fatal flaw or an aberrant personality that only the most objective being would notice. I quickly dismissed any thought of a fly being in the ointment and returned to the state of bliss fantasizing about our wedding. Yes, indeed, I accepted falling in love with a near perfect man and walking down the aisle in a lovely dress made of ivory silk with a few silk ribbon flowers embroidered around the hemline. I would ask Karma to apply my makeup and have Johns on hand to arrange my hair without too much ceremony and hair spray. I looked beautiful in my mind but worried, this too, might be an overblown creation existing only in my imagination. Maybe, I needed a professional to examine the inner workings of my mind, but did I really want to know what was in there, and upon further consideration, I realized whatever lurked there gave impetus to my artistic expression so should not be scrutinized too closely lest it go away in the process. If this should happen, I would not be me. Sometimes, too much thinking made my head hurt.

I decided to concentrate on the upcoming show. I had finished the painting of Lambert and was pleased with the outcome. Actually, I considered that an understatement. I loved the painting and didn't want to part with it but knew once it hung on the gallery wall, some stranger could come along and buy the rendering of my most precious companion. This thought surprised me. I knew a would-be husband was considered a woman's most precious companion, but it was hard to trust a man when my dog had already proved himself to be the most loving being ever to grace my life. Even, my own mother didn't think I was worth enduring the grief of loss to spend extra time with her daughter.

Again my head hurt from thinking too much. I needed to give it a rest, so I began packing the finished canvases to be picked up by the gallery van the day after tomorrow. Lambert helped by shoving crates aside after I had packed each canvas in its own crate. He even flipped them on their sides to lean against the wall. His ability to take charge and get the job done always astounded me. I don't know why since I had Mr. Dodder's words in my ears reminding me Lambert was a working dog and had more intelligence than most people he had come across. The last part had been said in a cynical voice; I assumed life held little enchantment for my crotchety neighbor, and so I gave little credence to his actual words. Now, of course, I nurtured a different view of Lambert's abilities. I believed he could do anything he set his mind to. I then envisioned him walking down the aisle carrying a little pillow with Daniel's and my rings tucked inside. Yes, Lambert would definitely make a beautiful ring bearer. I then wondered if he would insist on wearing plaid. I hoped not.

I spoke to Lambert about attending the gallery opening. I looked into his big brown eyes and saw an eagerness there to step out into the social art world. I realized I may be projecting here, but I really felt Lambert's thoughts fluttering inside my mind while I spoke of all the excitement that goes along with the unveiling of a new series of art. I told him about the art critics who would, no doubt, want to interview him since he was the first live being to ever appear on my canvas. He seemed even more pleased, but I did keep hearing the word Jack and again I thought it might be a projection on my part. I had already put Sally and Mr. Dodder on the guest list so an invitation could be extended to Jack without much fuss. I trusted Lambert implicitly to be on his best behavior, but I had no idea how Jack would conduct himself around a buffet table of finger foods and petit fours. I knew he had been on a bland diet so he might be feeling peckish and wipe out the prawn platter, stick his head in the punch bowl, and cleanse his palate with a few lemon cookies. My head became dizzy from all the chaos that could be created by one little dog. I made another mental note to ask Sally to dress Jack in his best leash and hold onto it.

Lambert had worked so hard helping me pack the canvases that I decided to take him to Karma's shop for a treat of his favorite baked goods. We hurried out the door in our usual effort to get to the car before Mr. Dodder's tongue flew over the fence.

"Heddy, yuh gonna make a girl outta him if'n yuh don't let him have a few male friends."

"But Mr. Dodder, Jack is Lambert's best friend so don't see there's a problem."

"Jack ain't much of a dog so far as I can tell. Looks more like a door stop than a dog and hangs off Sally's skirt like a real mama's boy. Not a good enough example for Lambert."

"But Lambert loves Jack." The second Mr. Dodder stuck his head over the fence, Lambert went after him with a ferocity I had never seen before. I knew Mr. Dodder's words about his friend had upset him.

"Gotta temper. Have yuh new man take him down a peg or two." Mr. Dodder hardly winced when Lambert reached up to grab him by the throat.

"We can talk about it some other time. Hope to see you at the gallery tonight."

"Not dressing formal but looking forward to being there." I felt the need to bang my head against the steering wheel a few times but instead backed out of the driveway so fast I took out the two forsythia bushes growing along the side of my lawn. Later when I returned, I noticed they had been pruned and straightened. Mr. Dodder's handiwork, no doubt.

Karma insisted on helping me find a dress that would be suitable for an artist at her own show. She spent several minutes examining the clothes in my closet before declaring it a disaster area except for the few pieces she had found for me. She drove me to the same boutique but wondered why Lambert couldn't be left at home for a few hours. I already knew I suffered from separation anxiety but hoped Karma wouldn't notice. She kept talking to me about my need to trust Lambert to be left alone for a couple of hours and that it would be good for him. It never occurred to her the problem was mine and not Lambert's, although I was quite aware my dog liked to gadabout like a social butterfly mingling in different societies to satisfy his varied interests, including an intense study of the human species. And what better way to do this than to tag along with me.

I don't think he knew I was on to his expansive mental critiques of human idiosyncratic behavior. Sometimes, I could feel his disappointment in us, as though we weren't quite up to snuff and possessed little understanding of the importance of our environment. The other day I saw him trot after a man who had thrown a candy wrapper on the ground. Lambert picked it up and shoved it in the side of his leather boot. The man seemed embarrassed and took the candy wrapper to the nearest trash can. Lambert smiled at him and the man saluted with respect. Yes, my dog would have made a stellar environmental lawyer or possibly a forest preserve police officer.

I always tried to keep a low profile at my own openings in hopes of blending among the guests and listening to their comments. A small group had gathered at Lambert's painting where I paused to eavesdrop but I, too, had become smitten by the angelic being gracing my own painting. I felt as though someone else had painted it. I sighed over the possibility a buyer could offer the full price and take what I considered a priceless painting home with him where I would never see Lambert's likeness again.

"Wow, I would love to have this hanging over my couch," a voice from a slouched figure said.

"Yeah, it would pick up the color of your couch," a friend of slouched figure responded.

"That painting is a masterpiece and not a piece of motel art." The voice sounded familiar. I turned to look and saw Daniel standing behind the slouched figure and her friend. The two guests shuffled over to the canapé table and began pouring copious amounts of wine in several glasses.

"Thank you," I said. "I suppose I ought not to have been eavesdropping. Just listening for feedback."

"They're here for the free food and drink. Not exactly reliable art critics," Daniel said and then turned his attention back to Lambert. "He is extraordinary. What a brilliant idea to blur the plaid behind your subject. Great idea to even use plaid. You're so imaginative."

"Oh, I can't take credit for the background. That was Lambert's idea. I only tried to make it work with the subject."

"Really?" Just then Lambert appeared and stood to admire himself.

"Yes, I have to admit Mr. Dodder is right. Lambert really is super intelligent. He even helped me crate all the paintings." I scratched his head and then noticed Daniel had suddenly disappeared. Lambert and I stood a moment longer before he became surrounded by fans and photographers from the papers and magazines on hand to write reviews. I had been selling privately these past few years and turned down several gallery offers for one woman shows, which artists never do, pure folly on my part and a little bit of necessary isolation. However, for some reason my seclusion piqued the interests of the press so they had arrived to see for themselves if my art work had suffered without the benefit of reviews. Apparently not, since I saw the gallery owner had already put sold stickers on half my paintings with two more hours to go. I worried over Lambert's painting. The photographers kept snapping pictures of it and Lambert who posed for the camera to most resemble his painted likeness. And then the worst happened, a red sold sticker was put next to his painting and I all but burst into tears.

Daniel saw my distress and put his arm around me. I noticed he was smiling, which further annoyed my nerves. "I'm so upset. I want to go home. I should never have allowed this picture to be here." A tear fell down my face and dropped onto Daniel's hand.

"I bought the painting for you. I'm going to hang it in my house and we can look at Lambert as the noble dog we both know him to be. I bought it for your wedding present. Will you have me? If not, you can have your painting with my love." He spoke with such earnestness, although I was slightly distracted when feeling Lambert's nose run up the side of my pretty new dress. Lambert then stood on his back legs and licked Daniel's face. How could I say no? So I said yes. Then I heard a loud clapping sound. I turned for a second and noticed the guests had all gathered around to hear Daniel's proposal. Even Jack stood eagerly next to Lambert, although I doubted he understood the subtext happening at an art show.

Everyone clapped and then dispersed to give us privacy, except for Lambert who leaned against me and wept. Daniel took out his handkerchief and dabbed the tears from my eyes and then went to work drying Lambert's tears.

The gathering quickly turned into an engagement party with everyone raising a glass of wine to toast the happy couple plus one. Even Mr. Dodder smiled with approval. He stood next to Sally looking like a normal almost attractive older man displayed in expensive dressy casual, no doubt, influenced by Sally's good taste. Jack stood brightly at the end of his leash appearing happy but slightly perplexed on why all the fuss. Lambert went over and ran his tongue up the side of his friend's face, which prompted Jack to shove his small, squat body against his comfortable friend. The moment would crystalize in my mind forever as being the most perfect moment of hope and happiness and the understanding life's journey is enhanced by having someone travel along with you.

10

LAMBERT WEIGHTS IN:

Sometimes, I set my mind to work trying to imagine what Mom's life was like before Yours Truly entered stage door right. The words drab and lonely came to mind but then again for all I knew she had been happily frolicking in a panorama of ethereal daydreams. The thought of not knowing something sobered me for a moment. I preferred to see myself as omnipotent. After all, herding dogs do have to be on constant alert and have an inherently high opinion of themselves, otherwise, they would lay around half the day fussing with their undercarriage. No, I felt a sense of importance by being front and center in Mom's life and seeing to it that she could ease herself from one day to the next while feeling loved by her favorite companion. Of course, I realized HH would soon try to shove me from this primo spot, but even when they're a happy couple living large on his farmette, her heart would always belong to the one who licked her face.

'There's no greater loyalty than a dog for his master'. I read that once on a cheap tapestry hanging in a Hallmark greeting card shop. I thought it greatly exaggerated a dog's lack of discernment when not taking into consideration dogs tend to choose where they want to hang their leash. Idiot

Farmer came to mind. I don't think he could inspire loyalty from the barnyard cats he let have the run of the outbuildings full of rodents.

I spent most of my week holding Mom's hand while she busied herself putting the final touches on my painting and packing all the others for her show. She seemed pleased and gave me extra helpings of food along with doggie bake goods. I could always be bribed with a dog scone hot from the oven and would do just about anything if somebody laid a baker's dozen on my plate. I know I thought about my stomach a lot but it seemed to feel better when full and allowed me to walk around the house with a self-satisfied smile on my face while listening to Jack harping on the dog grapevine about his mom going with that old codger next door to some kind of event that had excluded him. I got real busy and began dropping hints to Mom about inviting the little guy to the gallery opening. A shame he would have to stay at home while the old codger turned up with his mom and a set of empty pockets with no intention of buying anything.

Jack expressed periodic despair over having the old codger suddenly entering his life without previous warning. He got on the dog grapevine and honked constantly about the grizzled mating habits of the aged human male. He mentioned a great deal of groaning and sputtering, which resulted in a lackluster performance compared to the ones he'd seen on Animal Planet. I worried about Jack. Naturally, his flat face appearing at Mom's art show made me feel better over his not being left out. After all, sans balls, Jack was still twice the male as the old codger.

I spent some time at the party sitting with the little guy just to keep him company. Naturally, his attention went to the food table where any number of tidbits appealed to his deprived stomach. Maggie the Butcher continued to fill him with Pepto-Bismol long after his insides had quieted down. She put him on a diet of rice and beans, which caused him to fart a lot. I noticed when we sat together, the smell wafting from Jack's butt created a large circle of empty space around us and several disdainful looks from the art patrons. Mom rose above his emissions on this occasion and patted his head several times and called him a beautiful boy. While thinking this a gracious gesture on her part, especially since she was the guest of honor, I wondered about her ability to see beauty in Jack's face. I mean, the little guy looked like he'd got slammed in the face by a hard oak door. Not to mention, the flat part of his face was black while the rest of his body was a light tan color. Other than straining to breathe periodically from a tweaked nose, Jack made no mention of looking any different from those of us with a more traditional appearance. No, I gave him credit for having a certain cocky confidence about being one of nature's marvels rather than a fluke of nature. He did manage to control his natural inclination to wipe out the food table and waited for his mom to sneak him a canapé or two.

The old codger sure wore on Jack's nerves, though. We heard him waxing on about the integrity of Mom's art but worried it wouldn't sell because none of it looked like what it was supposed to be. We both got migraines from the stress of having to listen to the moron in residence. I managed to distract the little guy by telling him I would make sure he got all the left overs. This seemed to please him and he snuggled up next to me, which caused me an embarrassing moment. I mean two males cuddling in public wasn't the image I wanted to project, so eventually I convinced him Mom told me to mingle with the guests and excused myself.

I noticed most people wore black clothes. I quickly checked into the dog grapevine and discovered it to be a phenomenon in the East Coast urban areas when people stepped out their front doors for an evening spent among the intelligentsia. I wondered how the old codger fit into this scenario but noticed he did possess the wherewithal to wear tweed, the more collegiate look suitable for his pontificating nature. Although, I doubted his bullshit carried much weight with this crowd.

I took a moment to study Mom's painting of me. I marveled over how she had captured the essence of a working dog. Then I realized I must have conveyed a sense of purpose while sitting there chattering on the dog grapevine like a henhouse gossip. Well, I thought to myself, holding a pose for three hours felt like I had worked twelve, but still better than stepping in sheep shit to rescue one of their ungrateful brats. Mom came over and joined me. I noticed she began to cry and realized she regretted having put our painting at the risk of being sold to some stranger. Daniel joined us and then disappeared. I tried to stay by Mom's side but was mobbed by a group of fans. I wondered what they expected me to say. Nothing, I discovered. They just wanted to make a fuss over what a handsome dog I was and how well behaved. What did they expect I would do, pee on one of the freshly painted walls? Immediately, I thought of Jack on the other side of the room farting up a storm. If he hadn't been stuck to the end of his mom's leash, he could have gone outside for a bathroom break.

My fan club kept patting my fur and looking into my soulful eyes. I never thought anyone would call my eyes soulful. I preferred they appeared to be penetrating with intelligence. Soulful is the stuff of pouf dogs.

"Is he the cutest thing?" Skinny job in a tight black dress.

"Oh, and his soulful eyes." Skinny friend in black turtle neck with purple hair.

"Darlings, he does have the most divine hair." Johns.

"Wish I had hair like that?" Bald man.

"You do darling. Just not on your head." Johns.

Laughter.

I had heard enough and wandered back to Mom where she stood with her arms wrapped around Daniel, causing me to wonder what had prompted this turn of events. He had just bought our painting and was proposing marriage to us. I waited to hear Mom's answer. I could feel her body go stiff and then relax as she agreed to love him and live at the farmette where they could admire our painting together. A great deal of commotion followed this announcement, which caused Jack some confusion over the falderal, so I sat next to him and explained the concept of people marriage.

He looked at the old codger and his mom. Poor little guy. I knew exactly what frightening thoughts swept through his mind. I reassured him if things got unbearable at his house, we could always arrange sleepovers at mine. This cheered him up and we enjoyed the rest of the evening looking for handouts. I discovered soulful eyes had a certain advantage.

Everybody wanted to feed you if you looked at them with a sainted expression while managing not to fart from all the rich foods.

The three of us entered the back door after a series of unnecessary goodbyes from the old codger who had just pulled into his driveway with Jack and his mom in tow. I noticed Mom scrambled to get the key in the door before a disparaging word flew over the fence as a commentary for the evening's events, but Jack's mom grabbed the old codger by the arm and hurried him inside his own house.

The next thing I knew HH and Mom had made themselves comfortable on the couch shoved up together in each other's arms. I tried to join them with a great deal of stumbling around in an effort to find the most comfortable lap but my hairy butt wouldn't fit anywhere because they were practically on top of each other and in no mood to include me in their exuberance. Finally, I settled myself next to Mom and listened to the smacking and noisy reassurances of how much they loved each other.

"Heddy, I just can't believe this evening. I promise I'll make you the best husband." I found this declaration of love to be a sad disappointment coming from another male, nauseating even. Dogs didn't make fools of themselves over their females. They tended to get down to business and then move on to their daily routine.

"Oh, Daniel, I know you will. I'm so excited. Can Lambert be the ring bearer at our wedding?" My ears perked up when hearing the mention of my name. I saw myself decked out in Tartan plaid carrying two gold bands in the Scottish sporran strapped to my back. I cut a fine figure and felt confident I could make Mom proud.

"Yes, sweetie, anything you want, but we don't have to talk about wedding plans tonight. Why don't we move into the bedroom?" At this point, they both clung to each other like two victims of a sinking ship. The next thing I knew we're all tucked up in the large bed. My side had been reduced to a third of the bed instead of half, but I was perfectly willing to make the adjustment if it would add to Mom's happiness and after all Daniel might generate extra heat in the winter time to keep me and Mom warm during cold nights.

"Sweetie."

"Yes, darling."

"Do you think Lambert could spend some time on the other side of the door?"

"Is he crowding you?"

"Well, it's more that he's watching."

"He just wants to make sure you're not hurting me, but, of course, Lambert will understand. Come on, boy."

She's asking Moi to leave our bed instead of HH? I can't believe it, but I suppose if I were nuzzling a pretty female with the intention of mounting her, I would want some privacy. I graciously agreed to lay on the other side of the door for a couple of minutes, which turned into hours. Finally, they appeared now looking like rumpled bed clothes. Mom's hair stood straight up and smelled like HH's body sweat. The whole affair left me in a state of discomfiture. I then began to worry that HH would take advantage of Mom and make his forays into her bedroom a nightly event. If HH labored over this prospect, neither one of us would be getting any sleep. Eventually, he left and promised they would talk about wedding plans tomorrow night over dinner. We all said our goodbyes at the back door. I couldn't wait to get into bed. It had been a long week.

Next evening we went to the outdoor café where Mom and I had met that unfortunate man who wanted to smooth my rough edges by putting me in his obedience class. I didn't even know I had any rough edges to smooth previous to that unpleasant experience but now it was all behind us. We sat outside enjoying the evening breeze and drinking Pina Coladas but in my case a bowl of water with a lemon wedge and a little umbrella hanging off the side. Mom patted my head and kissed me with such affection, I knew she would never neglect her first love no matter how much effort HH put into making himself front and center in her life.

I glanced in his direction and was pleased to see him smile at me, a genuine smile of appreciation probably for bringing the two of them together. I realized at that moment the bedroom might be the only area Mom agreed to be without me. They held hands while feeding each other taco chips. I glanced around to see if anyone was watching this nauseating scene. Several eyeballs lit on me. I wondered what they found so fascinating about my appearance that it required considerable concentration. I glanced down at my coat to see if I had spilled some crumbs and licked my lips in case a few had stuck along the outside of my lips. Nope. I knew I didn't smell. The overzealous girly man Johns had tortured my hair with conditioner and other products to make me presentable to the show. Not to mention, the pedicure he insisted on giving me so I would have what he called 'a finished look'. If I had to actually do a hard day's work on a sheep farm, I would be laughed at by the barnyard animals and the farm hands would have a riot poking fun at my spoiled suburban life.

Finally, one of the other diners stood and approached our table. Mom and HH glanced up at him with worried expressions over the possibility this stranger intended to pull up a chair and sit down to jawbone for a while. Clearly not the case when they finally noticed he was staring at Yours Truly with a great deal of interest.

"I saw his photo in the morning paper. Lambert, is it?" the man said.

"Oh." Mom of little words.

"Yes. He was featured in the art section. Painted by the well-known but reclusive artist Heddy Lowe."

Nervous silence until HH finally found his tongue where he had last left it. "Yes, this would be Lambert. How may I help you?"

"Oh, I just wanted to buy the painting. Couldn't make the opening last night but was struck by that face." All eyes turned to Moi. I really wanted to take a swipe at the chip plate but thought it best to wait for HH to dispense with the intruder.

"I already bought it. Sorry, you're too late," HH said firmly.

"Oh, well perhaps, the artist will be using Lambert again. Your dog then? Commissioned work?"

"You might say that. Thank you for your interest. I'll mention it to the artist when I see her again." I could hear a dismissive note in HH's voice causing the man to scuttle back to his own table.

I then noticed Mom had hidden her face behind a menu during most of this exchange. She moved her chair so her back would be toward the stranger's table. "Thank you. I wouldn't have been able to handle all the questions especially about Lambert. He sounded rather obsessed with our dog." Several things went through my head simultaneously, someone being obsessed with me, the stuff of movies, and Mom referring to Yours Truly as our dog. My first instinct was to go over and get up into the man's face depending on the true nature of his intentions being whether he wanted to dognap me or felt so enamored by my painted likeness, he wanted to hang it on his wall. Both possibilities gave me a migraine, so I decided to drop all wayward thoughts and get busy having a go at the plate of nachos the waitress had just placed on our table.

"I hope you don't mind not having meat on these," HH said to Mom.

"No, of course not. I don't miss it at all, and I've been giving it some thought and have decided to become a vegetarian." HH smiled and reached for her hand. I stuck my paw on top of the pile of hands. This maneuver required me to stand on my chair and lean over the table. When returning to my chair, I picked up a healthy mouthful of nachos and laid them neatly on the little plate in front of me. I let them both admire my table manners for a second before gobbling up the Mexican torte.

We spent the next hour laboring over wedding plans. I grew restless sitting on a wooden chair listening to them discuss wedding cakes, flowers and Mom's dress. I only perked up when again Mom mentioned using me as the ring bearer. Fortunately, HH thought this a great idea and readily agreed with no mention of my Scottish sporran and the Highland Plaid. I had spotted in a store near Karma's boutique where the dummy in the window had been decked out in a plaid kilt with knee socks and poufy hat. I had no intention of going over the top by wearing a skirt but would like to represent my heritage in some dignified way. After all, Karma will, no doubt, drag Mom from store to store until finding the right gown for what I understood to be the most cherished day of the female human's life. I practically had to have the dog grapevine channeled to me in order to keep up with the meaning of all the happy couple had planned.

Eventually, my butt began to hurt from the hard chair so I jumped down unnoticed and took a moment to stretch my legs. The bushes looked inviting; I went over and peed on a few and then decided to circle the block at a rapid clip to get the kinks out of my joints. I realized I sounded geriatric, but really Border Collies were never bred to sit around café tables making wedding plans. I needed another job to occupy my time and keep me at the top of my game. It occurred to me Mom would be spending a great deal of her time snuggling up to HH at least until even she grew restless and wanted to get back to work. I would have to amuse myself until then.

The air felt good against my face as I traversed the commercial part of town and my legs screamed from happiness at being let loose to move at a gallop past all the pedestrians moseying down the busy street. I circled the block several times before running into the frightened faces of Mom and HH waving from across the street. I leaped over the hood of two cars before stopping dead in my tracks to smile up at them. I noticed they weren't smiling. Mom stood sobbing loud enough to attract attention, no more hiding behind a menu, but a public display that would probably embarrass her later when she pulled herself together.

"Lambert, you frightened us half to death. If you wanted to go for a good run, we'll let you loose on the farm but don't go off like this. You could have been killed. Do you understand, boy?" Even HH had a tight expression of worry on his face, causing me to believe he might be growing fond of Yours Truly. Mom had her arms wrapped around me and continued sobbing against the side of my neck. I leaned against her and tried in an awkward movement to put my own arm around her. A small crowd of onlookers had gathered to give their uninvited opinions, and then I heard the familiar voice of my new fan.

"I'll give you $10,000 for that dog."

"He doesn't have a price tag." HH practically barked these words. The man handed him a card.

"If you change your mind, I'll give you 20 grand."

"What's your problem, buddy? I told you he's not for sale."

"I'm sorry. I've just never been so taken with a dog before and well, friends do tell me I have more money than brains."

"Your friends have a point. Look, there are lots of dogs needing homes at the Udopt pet shelter. Check them out."

"I will. Thank you."

HH packed everybody in his Jeep and drove back home in silence with the occasional sounds of Mom whimpering into her hanky. I reached up from the backseat and patted her head once in a while in an effort to keep her calm. I felt like table scraps over all the heartache I had caused just because I wanted to enjoy a good sprint. When we returned home, Mom went inside and HH took hold of my leash and told me to lead the way. Three hours later, I dragged his lifeless body back home where he kissed Mom goodnight and nuzzled my head and mumbled something about male bonding, and then he left.

Mom and I snuggled up in the big bed. I could hear her sigh from contentment, which made me happy. Even though, HH panted the last mile home, I still thought he would make a nice addition to our little family. I realized Mom and I had to accept the whole package, which seemed to include the two fur balls and the periodic arrival of a neighboring horse. I discovered the horse kept running away from home and shutting himself in HH's little barnette in an effort to have a few solitary moments of contemplation. The grapevine animals considered him to be some kind of sage. I decided not to tax my mind thinking about the ramifications of having a resident know-it-all, but perhaps, he would come in handy for the occasional council when my thoughts became too muddled for me to wade through.

My heroic, older brother came to mind and weighed me down with the possibility of his not finding similar living accommodations as myself. I could hardly bear the idea of Idiot Farmer having kept him on the farm with the other overworked dogs but even if he sold him, invariably the highest bidder for a Border Collie always came from sheep farmers not suburban homeowners. They tended to have no clue as to what they were getting themselves into when taking on one as the docile, stay-at-home family pet.

I decided to check with Harry in the missing persons department at the downtown precinct. He asked more questions than I could answer and wanted an odor sample and last known address and when I couldn't supply either, he asked me if I were riding north or south when Apple Lady drove me to her home, and when I couldn't even come up with a definitive answer, he asked me if the sun was shining. "Yes, Harry, damn it right into my face at 11 o'clock in the morning lasting at least a full hour before arriving at my new home," I said. He seemed satisfied with this answer and got busy with his map and compass. A few minutes later, he got back on the dog grapevine, he told me to find Route 95 and run along the side of the road going north until coming to the familiar smell of Idiot Farmer's sheep farm. When I asked him where he thought Route 95 might be, he said to follow the smell of gasoline and cars packed with vacationers but not to get in any of their cars. He told me to stay out of sight of all human persons, otherwise, I might find myself in the dog pound waiting for a fate worse than sheep herding. I didn't like the sounds of this last bit, but decided if ever I got the gumption to get off my hairy butt and find my heroic, older brother, I would follow Harry's instructions to the letter.

I fell asleep with visions of my great adventure saving my heroic, older brother and only woke up once during the night to pull the down comforter up over my shoulders when noticing the central air conditioner must have been set on high.

11

Karma fell all over herself when I told her about our wedding plans. Again, she locked the boutique with Lambert clamoring at the window surround by a display of stuffed toys. He desperately wanted to come along with us. I just couldn't understand why Lambert's presence would disturb anyone. Finally, Karma called the uptown wedding gown store and told them the situation and something about money not being an object, and so apparently they relented and back we went to pick up a happy Lambert. I knew he would behave himself and that all he wanted was to be included. I had no idea he had plans of his own.

Once we settled ourselves in what they called the 'viewing room', several models walked by wearing the most gorgeous gowns I had ever seen, all white and lacy with lots of flounce, totally wrong for my body and lifestyle. When I told Karma this, she said lifestyle has nothing to do with wearing a dress on a girl's most important day. Yes, I agreed, but not over the top and besides that, I was no spring chicken, either.

"Do you have anything that drapes against the body in ivory with some 1940's romance to it?" I asked the store clerk. I could hear Karma gasp. Several minutes later a model appeared in just that style. Lambert barked twice to let me know he agreed on the selection.

"But Heddy, don't you think it's a little simplistic?"

"It's exactly me. Simplicity, itself. Even Lambert thinks so." We both looked at Lambert. He had wandered over to a male dummy outfitted in formal Scottish attire complete with sporran. While I was being measured for my dress, Lambert sat and studied the mannequin. When I had finished and put my clothes back on, I turned to grab Lambert's leash but he was busy behind the dummy. The thing kept weaving back and forth nearly tipping over and then suddenly its sporran fell to the floor and was quickly snatched up to dangle from Lambert's teeth. He stood on his hind legs and laid it carefully across the counter next to the cash register.

"Well, you did tell him you wanted him to carry the rings, and you know he has a penchant for plaid," Karma said and smiled.

"A sporran, though. I was thinking of an itty bitty basket or one of those satin pillow rings. Not a SPORRAN!" I could feel myself constrict from anxiety over the image of Lambert walking down the aisle looking like the dummy he had just pulled the man purse off of. Then I glanced over at Lambert and saw him sitting excitedly next to the counter, and I realized a good mother would never dampen such loving enthusiasm no matter how embarrassing. Besides if anybody could pull it off, Lambert could.

"Wrap it up please." Seconds after I relented and was in my purse searching for a credit card, Lambert had gone off and found a matching plaid hanky as big as a bath towel. Obviously, he wanted this tied around his neck instead of the lavender ones Johns does up after Lambert's weekly blow dry. So far, none of these hankies had ever made it to the car before Lambert had ripped them off and threw them in the nearest trash can.

"He sure has an unusual sense of his own identity," Karma said in admiration.

I bought the hanky, too, and resigned myself to having a Celtic ring bearer. I just didn't know exactly how to tell Daniel and when mentioning my concerns to Karma she said, "He won't care. He'll be too busy looking at you to mind what Lambert's wearing, but I would suggest having the best man practice taking the rings from Lambert's purse before the wedding." We both began laughing and even Lambert trotted along enjoying the gaiety of our raucous laughter.

Daniel suggested having the ceremony in a small chapel down the road from his property, invite only our closest friends, and have the reception catered at his house by a strictly vegetarian restaurant and make sure the cake was made without eggs, which he would arrange himself to take some of the burden off me. He seemed quite pleased with these suggestions, especially when he saw me smile in agreement; he seemed relaxed to the point of making me wonder what was wrong with my nerves. Why did I worry about every little thing including Lambert's own guest list? I knew he would want to invite Jack but would like Daniel's cats to be closeted in a room somewhere. He kept dragging me into the living room to take a look at how useless they were and why do they have to lay around and sleep all day on a couch that was big enough to accommodate his body. He looked at me and shook his head in despair over their lackadaisical easy way of going about their day. I watched him nose them to one end of the couch and position himself on the other ninety percent. They seemed to take Lambert's bossiness in stride but occasionally hissed at him when he tried herding them into the large bed at night along with Daniel, me and himself. They simply preferred the couch, which required Lambert to go and check on their wellbeing once in a while. He seemed quite put out at the inconvenience.

One day while talking about wedding plans, Lambert took his sporran out of its bag and tossed it in Daniel's lap.

"What's this?" he looked at the thing as though he were going to be asked to wear it.

"Oh, I forgot to mention Lambert wants to use it to carry our rings down the aisle." I actually didn't forget but couldn't bring myself to unveil yet another one of Lambert's little idiosyncrasies.

"Wow, boy, what a great idea". Lambert sat in front of Daniel who was sitting on my couch and smiled excitedly over his approval. "Have you tried it on him, sweetie?"

"No, not really." I sighed quietly, but I could tell Daniel was genuinely excited about the idea of Lambert going Celtic.

"My mother was from Scotland. She had the most wonderful brogue. I never tired of listening to her and would often ask her questions when I was a kid just to hear her talk." Daniel became quiet. I glanced from the dining area and saw his face buried against Lambert's neck. His mother died when Daniel was only twenty, killed in a car accident, and his father died a few years later from cancer. Needless to say, I felt quite small when realizing the flood of memories Lambert's 'penchant for plaid' must have prompted. I still hadn't figured out what to do with the big hankie, and so thought I wouldn't mention it to Daniel, yet. Just then, Lambert left the room and came back with it hanging from his mouth. He also tossed this in Daniel's lap.

"Oh, Heddy, how wonderful. I can take him to my tailor and have the sporran made more secure with a harness. My tailor is a Scot by the name of MacFarland. Lambert's just brilliant, Heddy. Brilliant. We're so lucky. I think even Isabel and Philomena appreciate him." Again Daniel wrapped his arms around Lambert's neck and buried his face against the soft part of his fur. Lambert ate this up, of course, and glanced back at me with an expression of absolute glee.

A week later, I sat in the back room of Karma's shop and quivered from anxiety. I had no idea what was wrong with me. Lambert crowded himself on my bean bag and shoved his body against mine while at the same time licking my face like it needed a good scrubbing.

"I think you have wedding jitters," Karma said and handed me a tissue. She spoke softly about her own wedding day. She spent most of it in the bathroom soaking in mineral salts and drinking Tequila from the bottle. "It felt like someone was nailing the lid shut on my coffin."

"I don't feel quite that bad and definitely don't need a shot of Tequila to calm my nerves. Actually, I have no idea what I am feeling except it's like I'm inside of my own body trying to get out."

"Same difference. You're just more articulate. That's exactly what's going on. Feel the need to run away from yourself because yourself may be doing something unfamiliar like marrying a man, leaving your own home, and living in his house, and wondering just how much of your freedom you really are giving up. And near as I can tell, you only care about two things, Lambert and painting. So long as you have those two things, it really doesn't matter whether you are married to Daniel and where exactly you live."

"You're right. It really is that simple. I can't imagine Daniel coming between me and Lambert and right now he's busy adding an addition to the back of his house for my studio. He even hired an expert to make sure the lighting is perfect for painting."

"See there. You feel better?"

"Much better, Karma. Until meeting you, I didn't realize how important it is for a woman to have a girlfriend. I've mostly just talked to Johns. He understands a lot about girl things and feelings."

"Of course he does." Karma smiled and patted mine and Lambert's head before leaving to go wait on a customer.

Lambert stopped polishing my face and began studying my expression. I smiled and he licked the edges of my lips and gave a quiet bark from happiness. He threw himself on the floor and rolled over for me to scratch his stomach, which was an uncharacteristic move for him. When I bent down to run my hand over him, he reached up with both paws and pulled me to the floor to tumble around for a while in a playful romp.

The magical day arrived all too soon. Karma and I stood in one of the ante rooms off the chapel lobby while Lambert,

Daniel and Daniel's publisher who would be his best man prepared themselves in another room. Everything had gone smoothly during the rehearsal. Even Lambert managed to march down the aisle instead of his usual trot. No problems with the best man and Daniel's smile helped to put me at ease. Johns had wanted to be my maid of honor, but I chose Karma instead only because I knew she could blend in while wearing a dress and Johns would go over the top and wear something borrowed from Cher's closet. I reminded him at this point his talents would be best put to use by doing something with mine and Lambert's hair, not to mention, I had no one to give me away and would he do me the honor. Johns became ecstatic over this role and kept calling it the most prestigious honor he had ever received since being appointed a Knight of the Flowers in his all men's group. I had no idea what this meant but was pleased to see him so happy.

My nerves seemed to take on a life of their own. I could hear them clanging against each other. I had tossed back a remedy earlier in the day to help calm them, but they still insisted on fighting among themselves right before the biggest moment of my life.

"Heddy, are you sure you don't want a shot of tequila?" Karma asked as she pulled a full bottle from her purse.

"No, absolutely not. I can't smell of liquor when the preacher says kiss the bride. My new husband would think he had just married a lush." I realized I had barked at Karma but quickly apologized just as Johns took the bottle from her hands and poured himself a drink. Fortunately, he had already finished my hair, which I kept admiring in the mirror. I had no idea what Lambert looked like. Daniel had been keeping him out of view all morning. Perhaps, that was one of the reasons my nerves seemed shaken. They felt better when Lambert was nearby and so did I, for that matter. Karma and Johns seemed a poor second compared to the company of Lambert and for a moment I dwelled on this thought and wondered what was wrong with me. I wondered if all people became dependent upon their dogs or if they just saw them as another member of the family to be fed, housed and clothed, the latter caused me to laugh out loud. No, only Lambert would be fussy about his wardrobe and demand that it be coordinated and reflect his Highland back ground. I marveled over his being tied to the side of the road one minute and the next he's picking out his own accessories with a very definite sense of style. I laughed harder and then noticed Karma and Johns were staring at me, their faces tilted slightly in concern.

"You all right. What's so funny?" Karma asked.

"Lambert. I wonder what he looks like," I said.

"Oh, I've seen him. Enough to make a mother proud. You'll be pleased. He's been practicing." Johns slurred his words and then I noticed half the tequila bottle was empty. I grabbed the bottle from his hand and threw it in the trash can.

"Practicing what?"

"Preacher will find that in the trash can. Sure you want to leave it there? I can take it outside." Johns offered.

"Practicing what, Johns?"

"Walking down the aisle. That's what he's been doing while you've been in here dressing. You do look beautiful, Heddy."

"Thank you. How does he look?"

""Well, let's just put it this way, you'd think he was the one who's getting married."

"Oh, but he is, Johns. So far as Lambert is concerned the three of us are getting married today not just Daniel and me. Lambert's been planning this day ever since Daniel passed his inspection," I said earnestly. They both looked at me like I suffered from a loose screw, but I had come to know what's in my dog's heart. Yes, Karma was right so long as Lambert and painting occupied the greater part of my life, I could ease myself through the days to come.

"Ah, well, he's perfect then, Heddy. You all look so beautiful." Johns dabbed at his eyes with one of his lavender hankies he had just taken from a smart-looking Armani suit. The man never ceased to surprise me. I hugged him and then Karma hugged me, and we all stood in a tight little circle until the music began. Karma opened the door and glanced down the aisle to see the minister, Daniel, and his best man waiting for us. The wedding march began and Karma held her bouquet and proceeded down the aisle first while all eyes looked back at her. Next the opposite door opened and Lambert appeared in full Highland gear. The tailor had created a dog vest out of the big plaid hankie and attached the sporran to the back. Lambert held his head high and when he began marching slowly down the aisle, I noticed his ensemble had been finished with white socks and small black shoes on each foot. So taken with the sight of my dog in full Highland regalia, I nearly forgot why I was there until feeling Johns move my elbow in the direction of my dog. I could have cried at that moment and then I lifted my head to see Daniel smiling with such happiness over the prospect of our little family being joined in holy matrimony; I could feel my nerves sigh from the very same happiness. The ceremony seemed a blur of words and promises, Lambert stepping up to have the rings removed by the best man who saw to it they all went to the appropriate fingers. Not until we kissed, did I feel truly married, happy and overcome with emotion and then Lambert taking direction seriously stood on his back feet and rested one paw on Daniel's shoulder and the other paw on mine so he could easily join in and give each of us a gentle lick. Then I heard a roar of clapping from our wedding guests, and so we turned to run after Lambert, back down the aisle and out the door to stand and wait for congratulations and pictures.

12

Lambert Weighs In:

Mom and HH finally came around to seeing my world view of life being better lived if it's lived under one roof in harmony and love for the one who possessed the vision of knowing this. The latter, of course, would be Yours Truly. Certainly, I out did myself at our wedding when gliding down the aisle a sight too wondrous to behold followed by Mom, a vision of loveliness herself. I could wax on sounding like a 19th century romance novelist but the fact is my hairy butt grew tired of waiting in the wings to make an entrance, the little girly shoes pinched my toes, and I was dependent on one of the church deacons to keep my socks pulled up. However, the happy expression on Mom's face made my efforts worth the extraordinary lengths I had to go through to get done up in formal attire befitting someone of my background.

A harrowing moment had occurred at the tailor's when the old man got out a pair of shears big enough to cut through a wheat field. I thought he intended to have a go at my balls with them, and so naturally I jumped off the fitting platform and ran half way to Rhode Island before HH caught me. He seemed to understand the cause of my anxiety, although a good whiff told me he still had his own balls intact, prompting me to wonder if he would be dusting them off to use for their natural purpose to procreate the human species. I hoped not. If he had the ability to understand what I was saying, I could tell him what a drain on our natural resources another human would be. The disposable diapers alone would add to our country's biodegradable nightmare. Not to mention, the idea of sharing Mom with anyone else held little appeal.

Daniel coaxed me back to the scissor wielding tailor's to be properly measured and fitted for my vest. I had never worn one on the sheep farm so had no idea what MacFarland kept going on about when mentioning buttons running down the front, no Velcro, and a tam, which HH declined by telling the old man he didn't want anything to detract from my dignity. However, when they both came up with the nonsense of my wearing shoes, my dignity seemed to be left by the wayside but at least while poring over the catalog, they both declined the shoes that laced up to a man's hairy knees. HH must have felt me wince over the image of my own hairy legs being done up in a series of crisscrossing straps double knotted just below the edge of my white crew socks. While studying the Celtic catalog, I thought of Johns and wondered why he didn't buy his skirts from the men's department instead of flouncing about the salon in something that looked like it came off the nearest Lane Bryant mannequin. Fortunately, he spared us from guessing his gender most of the time by wearing a pair of bib overalls circa 1970s. He kept going on about wanting to dress retro and then got upset when Mom told him he was retro. I have no idea what she meant exactly, but I could smell Johns' aggravation over this remark and felt his pain. Sometimes, Mom surprised me with her lack of sensitivity, but then I remembered she picked me up off the side of the road not knowing a thing about my living habits. This thought always made me sigh with contentment.

While in my little musty room with the church deacon, I could smell Mom's anxiety, along with a whiff of alcohol strong enough to calm a bull elephant, and Johns' lavender perfume fighting with Karma's musky scent. The church deacon smelled like moth balls and horehound drops. I worried about Mom and hoped when seeing me, she would pull herself together and enjoy the festivities. I could feel her longing to have me nearby for comfort. Johns and Karma must be absolutely useless as sounding boards. Between the two of them they had enough opinions to run a small country. Then I heard the music and knew it was time to carry the rings down the aisle.

When the door opened and I saw Mom, I had to squash the impulse to run over and lick her face for comfort. Nope, like the true working dog I was bred to be, I marched down that aisle with all eyes on me in admiring glances. I could have been mistaken for the bride what with all the oos and ahhs that filled the vaulted room. I wanted to wait for Mom but my instructions had been to arrive at the altar and stand next to HH's friend who would be taking the rings from my sporran. I really loved my new vest and hoped Mom would let me wear it again. I made a mental note to bury the shoes somewhere in HH's field, so the happy couple wouldn't drag them out again and make me wear them to the next big shindig. I hoped to yank them off my feet the second we made it back to the farmette where all the food was being prepared for the wedding guests.

Fortunately, the ceremony only lasted a few minutes before HH's lips were planted on Mom's and then I joined the family circle of love. I could practically feel my heart leap with joy. The only thing missing was Jack. I supposed my thoughts should have wandered to the silly fur balls but Jack felt more like family and after all he was my best friend. I knew he sat on the last pew with the old codger and his mom. I could feel his eagerness to join me, but I could also smell his restraint. I tossed him a happy glance when I trotted back down the aisle and out the church door.

Once at the house, everyone forgot about Yours Truly the ring bearer, which left Jack and me free to gather up my shoes and find a remote area to bury them. We chose the back corner of the property line and began digging. Jack took to this task like a stunted backhoe and had gone down three feet in no time. We figured that was way beyond a human's ability to smell shoe leather and so felt assured HH would never find them. I further camouflaged the burial site by planting a few weeds in the loose dirt. Once satisfied, we agreed to go back and check the floor for crumbs. Jack's stomach growled constantly from hunger. Poor bastard, I thought. Maggie the Butcher was relentless in keeping him in starvation mode while his plumbing healed.

"Hey, Little Guy, wait up. Let me give you a sniff." He stood stock still while I ran my nose along his underside. Nope. Not a hint of inflammation anywhere. I told Jack we would fill his stomach to the brim with the best on the buffet table. He knocked up against me in appreciation and together we high tailed it back to the house to scope out the situation.

Jack hadn't spent much time with cats and asked exactly what they were good for. I didn't have a real answer to this question and nearly said adornment until seeing Isabel had a wad of chewing gum stuck in her fur, no doubt, put there by someone's little brat. It fell to me to help with this knotty problem. Jack tagged along as we all crowded in the big bathroom. Isabel took pride in her long orange fur coat; needless to say, her present predicament had her in such a tizzy she dove in the bathtub and tried to dislodge the gummy mess by having a go at it with three of her four paws. After discovering this exercise to be useless, she threw herself backward and lay limp as a tree sloth. I burrowed my nose into her fur and yanked the thing out with my front teeth. Philomena and Jack watched in stunned silence. Now, I had the disgusting wad in my mouth and not knowing quite what to do with it, I knocked the toilet lid up and hacked the thing in the water and then flushed it down the bowl. Just then, Philomena jumped in the bowl and nearly went down with it. Fortunately, we herding dogs were also bred to save lives as an instinctive reaction otherwise I might have let her keep going, but no, I grabbed her just as the water disappeared down the toilet and flung her wet body into the bathtub with her dazed sister.

"They aren't smart like dogs." Jack said as he peered over the side of the tub. Four eye balls stared back at him with disdain.

"Smart enough to get what they want," I said and leaned over the tub and began washing both of them, which surprisingly they didn't mind and actually seemed pleased I would make the effort.

Just then one of the wedding guests opened the door and screamed in surprise at the small animal kingdom gathered there. This frightened both fur balls, who climbed the shower curtain and threw themselves out the window. The commotion caused Jack's nerves to give way resulting in a small puddle of pee on the floor, which I quickly covered with the bath mat. I stuck my nose against his butt and shoved him out the door before the rest of the party appeared to investigate the ruckus.

That problem solved, we decided to check the buffet table. Fortunately, a stool had been placed at the far end for no apparent reason except to allow me to maneuver myself up on it and have a good look at the food display. I knew Jack loved cheese so I picked up a mouthful and dropped it over the back side of the table where he stood waiting. I then gathered up half the neatly stacked fake weenies and tossed those over, accompanied by several cookies. A caramel jelly roll affair had been sliced and placed on vegan plates that could be eaten when finished with the real food. This eco invention boggled the mind with its redundancy. A tree leaf would do the job just as well without all the industry needed for manufacturing something designed to make the green people feel better about not polluting the environment. Never mind, what it took to power the machinery that made their vegan dinnerware.

Jack and I slowly sniffed out our favorite foods from this messy pile and then lay under the table to take a quick nap until the newlyweds finished the cake cutting ceremony. Occasionally, I reached my paw up and pulled down a few more pieces of organic raw cheese bought from a farm that hand-milked their cows. I had heard HH telling Mom the importance of calling the farms to find out how they treated their animals and said he had gone so far as to show up uninvited at the farm where his milk products were produced. I told Jack this and we had a good laugh. The little guy did have a sense of humor. You got to love him for his wherewithal to see the zaniness going on around him. Just then the tips of the old codger's shoes appeared underneath the edge of the table cloth.

I could feel Jack quiver and laid my paw on his back to calm him. We waited. The shoes moved up and down the table for several minutes, no doubt, lingering over each savory choice. Jack gave me one of his hang dog looks. I felt sorry for the little guy and really wanted to take a bite out of the old codger's shoes but the screams would ruin Mom's party and call attention to mine and Jack's unauthorized smorgasbord. Finally, they left only to return seconds later to fill two glasses with HH's special apple/pineapple juice punch without the real punch as I heard one of the guests commenting when being disappointed the bowl hadn't been filled to the brim with two quarts of hundred-proof vodka.

Jack began a long monologue on the dog grapevine alerting all of his friends about the elderly shadow looming large over his life and bringing an oppressive, disapproving aspect to his every waking moment, which previous to this event had been pretty happy-go-lucky. I, personally, don't remember the little guy being happy-go-lucky the first time I had met him in Maggie the Butcher's waiting room. I do remember him clamoring to get in his mother's purse when being stalked by a Rottweiler. Sad to say, but I believed the old codger's presence in Jack's life was less ominous than a dog who could snap him in two without a second thought. Not that Jack was making much ado about nothing; he had a point in wanting to live without all the monitoring. He finished his diatribe with a few last words about life without hope was a life unlived. These mismatched sentiments brought a chortle to my lips, but I choked them back and waited for the final wrap up, which included the vision of himself taking to the road with a knapsack and his mom's portable GPS to wander the highways and byways. Poor bastard, I thought, and was relieved when the old codger's shoes finally left.

Just then, the cake cutting ceremony began. Mine and Jack's ears went forward with noses in the air waiting for all the guests to receive their vegan plates laden with the soft lemon chocolate concoction that made a dog's mouth water from anticipation. These festivities took about an hour with only a few crumbs falling on the floor. Then, finally, we could see the caterer's big white shoes moving along the bottom edges of the table cloth. When finished slicing the cake and handing it to people, her shoes left, and I felt it was safe to get a couple of plates for me and Jack, but to my surprise, two large China plates were being shoved under the table. I licked the tips of Mom's fingers and she patted my head. Never had I loved a being as much as I loved Mom. She thought of me in the midst of what Karma called 'the most important day of a girl's life'. After we finished eating our cake, I slid from under the table to go sit next to Mom. She rested her hand on the side of my face and pulled my head against her new dress. She hadn't even minded the smudge of chocolate coming off my lips onto her new dress. She looked down at me and smiled with love. I could feel myself smile. And then they were gone.

Jack and I found ourselves alone at the farmette tended by his mom and the old codger. I couldn't believe we had babysitters, especially ones who were too old to do anything but sit on the back patio and look at the sunrise or at least that's what I hoped when my mind took a sudden left turn to imagine them mating when the night came. No, Jack and I hurried outside to have a conference over this turn of events. I wailed about being stuck with someone who would like nothing better than to put me to work mowing the back forty. Jack looked at me with great sympathy and then whimpered. We both agreed it would be best to keep a low profile. I then glanced over and saw Thomas Jefferson in the small barn. I dragged Jack over to meet him. Perhaps, he would have a few words to say on the subject.

Thomas Jefferson opened the door and let us inside the barnette. I was surprised to notice the well-finished interior of this small building. HH had even put in a camp bed for his imaginary farm hand along with a small table and chair, photos of his book covers hung on the wall along with one of me and Mom smiling at each other. My heart fluttered at the sight of a memory long gone but important enough for my new step dad to put on one of his walls. Jack and I made ourselves comfortable on the camp bed and began to ask the horsey sage for advice on how to survive the two days ahead. I remembered Mom saying they would only be gone for two dark nights.

"Close your eyes and let the stillness pull you into the night on the other side and listen to the sound inside instead of the voices you cannot quiet on the outside. You will begin to enjoy the inner peace brought about by the silencing of your mind."

Jack and I fell asleep on the camp bed after enjoying two seconds of guided meditation and woke up when hearing our names being called for dinner. We thanked Thomas Jefferson and then left him contemplating the silence or whatever sages do when they are left alone with their own wisdom. Jack and I would spend most of the next two days keeping a low profile on the camp bed when not out roaming the fields.

13

When we returned from our short honeymoon spent in Newport, Rhode Island, I noticed Jack and Lambert had taken all their bedding and made themselves comfortable in the small barn next to the house. I knew Lambert liked the coziness of HH's bed and wondered exactly what prompted him to prefer camping with the neighbor's horse. I could understand why Jack wouldn't want to leave Lambert and sleep with Mr. Dodder in whatever bed he had chosen for his own during our absence. Sally offered little explanation except to say both dogs seemed quite happy with their arrangement and since neither one seemed any worse for the wear, I let it go without too much worry.

Mr. Dodder went on about Lambert still not making himself useful around the house and even went so far as to accuse me of ruining a perfectly good sheep dog. Daniel stepped into the verbal fray and said he had given the matter a lot of thought and maybe what Lambert needed was a few sheep of his own. Then, of course, Mr. Dodder just couldn't let it go and told Daniel he would have no idea how to go about the task of raising and sheering sheep to sell their wool to the fiber industry. I began to get a headache and excused myself to unpack.

Sally came along with me. "Jack loves Lambert."

"I know," I agreed. "And Lambert feels the same way." Actually, I had no idea what I was talking about. For all I knew

Jack could be one of those friends who attached themselves to you for life whether you wanted them there or not. Although, the two seemed quite happy together and even leaned against each other when they sat outside on the grassy knoll to view the horizon.

"Would you let Lambert spend a few nights at my house with Jack? A doggie sleepover?" she asked.

Lambert came running from the other room and shoved himself against my legs and then stared at me with startled eyes. I took my cue well from his expression. "Oh, no. Not for quite a while. He has to get settled here. And remember he's had to make several adjustments when leaving the sheep farm, all of which have probably been traumatizing to the poor thing. I know you understand. But, certainly, you can drop Jack off here anytime so they can be together."

"Oh, you're right, of course. Jack would like that."

Lambert smiled and then jumped on the bed and licked my face. I missed him while away and a few times Daniel had to reassure me Lambert was all right in the hands of Mr. Dodder and Sally. I had my doubts but did owe some undivided attention to my new husband. We had gone on lovely walks on the paths above the cliffs aside the ocean, but occasionally I found my thoughts straying to Lambert and what a great time he would have scampering along with us.

When Sally and Mr. Dodder left with Jack, he whimpered and then ran back to Lambert, who bent down to nuzzle his little friend. I guess I wouldn't want to climb in the car with Mr. Dodder and spend a great part of my life listening to him pontificate on all subjects related to acceptable dog behavior. Just before Mr. Dodder moved his truck out of the driveway, he rolled down his window and told Lambert to get a job. Lambert lifted his leg and peed on his wheel cover and then walked back in the house to join Philomena and Isabel on the couch. He seemed both emotionally and physically exhausted. I wondered what had happened this weekend that would cause Lambert's spirits to be so low.

"Honey, do you think it was too much for Lambert to have Jack here an entire weekend?" We both stood in the living room and stared at the couch covered with piles of sleeping bodies.

"No, he loves Jack. I think it was too much having that old man here."

"Do you think we need to consider another babysitter? Who, though?"

"Really sweetie, is there anything Lambert can't do? I would trust him implicitly with the care of Isabel and Philomena."

"Oh Daniel, that's so sweet. You're right, of course. There's nothing he can't do except answer the phone when we want to check up on things."

"Should we decide to go away again, we'll put in a nanny cam and rig up an intercom so we can hear Lambert's responses when we ask about his day. He's very expressive I've noticed."

I began laughing and then Daniel caught what an understatement that was and he began laughing. Lambert glanced in our direction with one eye open and then sighed before going to sleep. He was definitely expressive all right.

We left him so we could continue unpacking and cleaning up after our company but everything seemed to be in place.

"Honey, I can't find Lambert's bed or his stuffed toys and portable water bowl," Daniel called from the other room.

"Oh, I meant to tell you, Sally said Lambert and Jack slept with Thomas Jefferson."

"Really? Let me see." We hurried to the barn and flipped the light switch. The place had acquired a homey dog feel to it causing us to deduce Lambert and Jack had spent the better part of two days holed up with the neighbor's wayward horse. "How odd."

"There must be a reason for them to have camped out here. Especially Lambert, a dog who really likes his comforts," I said.

"You don't think Mr. Dodder hurt him or Jack, do you?"

"No, of course not, only with words; this probably became quite tiresome for them both." We can wash all his stuff tomorrow. Let's call it a night." We went back to the house and moved along to the bedroom.

I loved my new studio. Floor to ceiling windows filled the backside with French doors in the middle that opened onto a small private patio where the Garden Shop had arranged numerous containers of flowering plants along with vines hanging over their terra cotta sides all the way to the newly laid brick surface. One lounge chair with a matching heavily cushioned bench had been arranged next to each other facing outwards. I knew Daniel intended this to be mine and Lambert's private area. Lambert lay on the bench now in a half-dazed slumber enjoying the sun warming his fur. I went outside and sat beside him in the lounge chair. Five seconds later, he was crowded next to me staring with a bored expression on his face.

"What do you want my sad beauty?" Lambert jumped down immediately and pulled the handle on the French door. He easily flipped it open and entered my studio. I made a mental note to have a security check done of the house. He then walked over and sat facing my easel in an elegant pose although somewhat stiff and slightly affected with the stone sheep he had dragged from the corner to complete this tableau. I knew, of course, he wanted to model for me again. I hadn't realized how much he enjoyed all those hours we spent together in the studio. In fact, now that I gave it some thought, Lambert seemed his happiest during our painting sessions whether they be in the fields or in my studio or for that matter whether he was actually glued to a spot or out bounding in the open country side. Lambert just liked being part of the whole process of painting together. Mr. Dodder, it pains me to admit, was right when saying Lambert needs a job but he also needs to be trusted enough to choose the right one for himself. Suddenly, I had this image of Lambert lying next to a chipped peeling fence with meadow grass growing around the posts. We could place the stone sheep in the foreground and see what happens with my paint brush. As though reading my thoughts, Lambert began moving the stone statue toward the door and ran back and picked up my paint bag and his water bottle which had been placed neatly next to all of Lambert's gear. I stopped for a moment to consider how lucky I was to have found someone as loving and thoughtful as Daniel. Lambert barked the moment this thought entered my head. This convinced me, without a doubt, Lambert could read my thoughts and there was probably no need for a great deal of verbal instruction on my part. I laughed, prompting Lambert to bark again and wag his tail from happiness.

I grabbed a wheel barrow setting empty in the yard and put all our paraphernalia along with the statue in it and off we went to find a dilapidated wooden fence. We roamed around the fields for a while until hearing Lambert barking up ahead. Sure enough when arriving a few feet behind him with the unwieldy garden transport, I spotted what caused Lambert to make such a fuss, the neighbor's split rail fence. It appeared perfect for Lambert's tableau. We set about arranging everything, stepping back to take a look, and then more arranging, stepping back again, and continuing this process until we were both satisfied with the final look. Then Lambert lay down and assumed a dignified but dreamy air, unusual for a working dog. I loved the dichotomy of it and was now convinced of my dog's brilliance. Just then my cell phone rang.

"Don't worry, Lambert and I are working near the wooden fence just west of the house. No, we don't need any chili right now, but later would be great. We've just got started. Love you, too, sweetie." Lambert yawned and looked away.

"Okay, Lambert, resume your pose." He immediately affected a dreamy air again, which further convinced me of my dog's genius. "We will have to remember to leave messages for Daniel the next time we take off, otherwise, he'll worry about us," I added. Then I began to draw.

Three and a half hours later, I had completed numerous drawings and had a general idea of where I wanted to place the stone sheep and what perspective I wanted to use. I showed the finished drawings to Lambert. He nosed through them and then stopped short when seeing himself with the stone sheep in the background on the other side of the fence. Again, he brought his paw down hard on this one. I had to laugh. It appeared as though the dog could care less about his charges or that he was so deep in thought that the reality of being a sheep dog had receded into the back ground of both his mind and physical world. A good art critic could do a thorough job on the dog's perspective, and say he was more than the sheep he was meant to herd, or that he was lying down on the job, or he had a jaundiced view of his work life being solidified into one identity, which had little to do with his own personal freedom or his true self. Yes, perhaps Lambert was onto something when choosing this one.

"Thanks, Lambert. Now, I want you to go and stretch your legs while I tidy up these drawings." I patted and kissed him. He trotted off to enjoy a good run. I loved watching him. I just sat there and watched him for a while before going back to studying the drawings. The one Lambert had chosen differed considerably from the others, an interesting choice I thought and for a moment I wondered if Lambert could learn to draw. I remembered seeing a short film of an elephant drawing a flower. What a lovely thought and then I, too, drifted off to enjoy my day dreams.

Daniel fixed us his specialty vegetarian chili and set three bowls at the table. I noticed Lambert and Daniel took the end chairs while I sat at the middle side. I wondered if this was male behavior in all species and then felt special when realizing I was flanked by my favorite beings. I had not gotten to know Daniel's cats, yet, but did want to nurture our relationships. Lambert seemed happy from putting in an afternoon of work followed by a good frolic in the fields. He now had the run of the property, which seemed to please him to no end. When finishing his bowl of chili, he jumped down and joined Philomena and Isabel on the couch.

"I found an auction house for livestock up a ways on 95. I thought maybe we could go and look at some sheep for Lambert. What do you think, honey?" Daniel said.

"Really? How does that work exactly? And how would we get them home?"

"I don't know. Maybe they deliver," Daniel responded.

"I know we told Mr. Dodder we would get Lambert some sheep, but he seems happy with his life and loves working with me. And he's great at setting up our back drop and taking it down." I noticed Daniel looking at me like I had said something odd. "I mean look what a great job he did modeling for our painting." We both glanced at the painting over the fireplace.

"Oh, I trust whatever you say, but maybe we could just take a drive tomorrow and check out the place. They might have a pamphlet on how to purchase sheep and what you do with them after you take them home," Daniel said this with such seriousness, we both began to laugh. I patted his hand and agreed; it wouldn't hurt to take a look at a few sheep and Lambert might like a nice outing.

We finished dinner and moved into the living room to be near our new family. I noticed Lambert tended to use the cats as a place to rest his chin. They didn't seem to mind, especially Isabel. She reached up and put her arms around his neck and licked the inside of his ear with more zeal than I could muster when washing my paint brushes. I wondered what brought about this change of attitude. Lambert didn't seem to mind and, in fact, I noticed he enjoyed the fuss she was making over him and even the other cat raised her head once in a while and licked Lambert on whatever part of his body that rested nearest to her tongue. Lazy didn't begin to describe Daniel's felines. I loved my new life and having someone in it who was actually interested in how I had spent my day. I had no idea marriage and family could be so comforting. I felt almost elated, but mostly I felt contentment as though, I finally arrived at a place I could truly call home. I restrained the urge to crowd onto the couch with all the fur bodies, but instead I sat with Daniel on the love seat and nestled against him.

Several hundred dusty sheep had been shoved into three corals and stood waiting to be bought and sold to the highest bidder. Lambert shocked both Daniel and me by refusing to get out of the car. We found ourselves in an odd dilemma and didn't know quite what to do. Neither one of us thought it was a good idea to leave Lambert alone in the car. Maybe if he were a poodle or some little piece of nothing like Charo, no one would notice or even care, but a genuine sheep dog would attract unwanted attention. A tall man wearing chaps and a cowboy hat strode toward us. I thought for a second I was in one of those gay night clubs Johns used to drag me to. He walked right past us and leaned into the window.

"What's wrong great buddy?" he asked Lambert, who ignored him and stared straight ahead. The man shook his head and turned to us for an explanation.

"He doesn't want to get out of the car," I said. "It's not like him. Usually Lambert enjoys an adventure."

"Well, this is not exactly an adventure for a sheep dog. It's a way of life, which makes his behavior seem peculiar." The man showed no signs of leaving.

"What's your interest?" Daniel asked, abruptly probably in an effort to get rid of the cow poke so we could deal with our own family situation.

"He looks familiar, like the dog leaving in that truck." The man pointed toward the biggest, shiniest truck I had ever seen.

Suddenly, Lambert shot out of the car window and chased after the truck down the road. Daniel and the cowboy ran after him. I jumped in our car and crept up on my running dog and threw open the car door and yelled for him to jump inside it was faster. Lambert did just that, and we took off after the truck but it disappeared amid the four lanes of traffic and three semis. I took the first exit and returned to find Daniel and the cowboy sitting on a large tree stump smoking small cigars.

"Sorry, great buddy. Must have been someone you knew." He patted Lambert, who sat forlornly in the front seat. We said goodbye to the cowboy and watched him walk toward the barn.

We decided to drive back home and take Lambert for a run in the fields. He still seemed sad as though suffering from the kind of grief that stuns your heart and causes your knees go weak.

14

Lambert Weighs In:

The smell of my heroic, older brother caused a recollection of early memories and the feeling of comfort I felt when we laid side by side and slept on a tattered plaid blanket with several of our scrawny brothers and sisters, wondering what the world was like beyond the barn door. The only time I ever felt at home happened whenever my brother put his arm around my neck and licked the top of my head resting on his tiny shoulder. I loved my heroic, older brother. He taught me how to drink milk from a bowl and hide in the piles of hay every time we smelled the tobacco rot odor mixed with year old sweat coming off of Idiot Farmer's clothes. My body shook so hard underneath the hay piles, heroic, older brother had to lay on top of me to keep the hay from moving. We could see the dried blood on Idiot Farmer's well-worn boots and were left to wonder exactly how it got there. I loved my brother and knew he was the only thing keeping me from ending up on the toe of Idiot Farmer's boot.

Periodically, his dilapidated wife would storm into the barn and point to us and yell at her husband about making a profit from the bitch's labors. We had no idea what she meant until noticing our brothers and sisters began disappearing on us and finally we were down to four and then just the two of us. Heroic, older brother taught me to tune into the dog grapevine and pay attention to what was being said in case we became separated from each other. Eventually, Idiot Farmer took my brother to the fields and left me to wander around the crab grass growing in his yard. His dilapidated wife kept telling me I would never amount to anything and after a few months of hearing her words and only getting the table scraps she threw out the kitchen window, I began to believe I really just might not amount to something worth using on God's green earth. I kept trying to hear my heroic, older brother on the dog grapevine, but he sounded too worn out to talk much about his day and then, eventually, I found myself tied to a table along the roadside, and I never heard from him again. Not until smelling the familiar comfort coming out the window of a shiny truck at the urban barnyard.

Mom let me lean against her on the way back home that day, stroked my head and spoke soothing words into my ear but nothing could bring me out of the depths of sorrow in knowing my heroic, older brother was out there somewhere, but I had lost my connection on the dog grapevine, which usually meant a dog was too busy to spend an afternoon jawboning to the idlers with their ears hung over the grapevine listening to a blow by blow account of each other's daily exploits.

I did get in touch with Harry at Missing Persons and described to him the highway and the barnyards full of sheep. He said again it sounded like a straight shot up route 95 but to keep clear of human persons if I decided to track my brother down, and then he reminded me to take food and water with me if possible, otherwise, he said to leave in the night on a full stomach. I had not made any firm plans about scouting the countryside to find my heroic, older brother. I knew Mom needed me to help her get through the days. One of the things I learned on the dog grapevine was many a happy marriage was held together by the love of a good dog.

Mom and I spent most of the winter months working with her paints. When the snow covered the ground, she took pictures of me outside in all sorts of crazy poses, and then she hung them up in her studio to copy the back ground on her canvas while I sat my hairy butt down in the desired pose and watched her play with her brushes. Since being an artist's model was mind-numbingly boring, I hung my ear over the dog grapevine and chatted with Jack. The old codger had made himself at home in Jack's life and spent a night or two with his mom while Jack fretted outside the bedroom door. He kept going on about the racket they were making and why wasn't his mom satisfied with just him in her life? Why did she have to bring in someone else to clutter up the house, especially an old man who had his mind firmly set on the way he thought everything ought to be done? Jack asked if he could move in with me or even live in the barn with Thomas Jefferson. Poor bastard was that desperate. I knew Mom had a big heart but didn't think she would interfere in Jack's world.

I loved my new home and could feel Mom's happiness buzzing all around her. She kept telling Karma how Daniel turned out to be the best husband and that she owed it all to Yours Truly. Mom said she didn't have a clue when it came to understanding a man, but that I had bypassed all her neurotic fears of living in the same house with one. She repeatedly talked to Karma about how clean Daniel kept the house and himself. She said he even bathed the hair balls every few months. I began to wonder about Mom's view of the human male. Why wouldn't they be like me, all neat and tidy about their under carriage. HH took two showers a day during the hot summer months and brushed his body with a dried sponge that looked like something he had found at the bottom of the ocean. He even trimmed the hair around my toes when we found ourselves in the bathroom together. Mostly, I followed HH in the small room to watch him go through the daily routine of squirting canned soap on his face and then scraping it off with a knife. I noticed he never went below his neckline, which left a great deal of hair on his chest, probably to keep himself warm. I gave this process a lot of thought and felt satisfied there wasn't a hair on my body I disliked enough to crop every day. I have to admit I appreciated the way HH kept my toes all nice and neat. The only difference he tried to make in Mom's and my lifestyle was to eliminate Johns as my hairstylist, which was all right by me. My nose took a beating every time I stepped through the salon doors to encounter numerous and conflicting smells. Mom, however, enjoyed our weekly beauty routine, which was exactly how she worded it to HH when my grooming came under discussion. I knew HH objected to the idea of my being treated like a pouf dog, which endeared him to my heart, but even I knew better than to interfere with Mom's calendar. The subject disappeared from the discussion table never to be brought up again. Actually, Mom, even though she took on a husband and his fur balls, didn't change our together time at all. We still went on our daily walks; she still cried into my fur on a bad day; and stroked my body with the love of a devoted companion. I wanted for nothing, except once in a while an image of my heroic, older brother would float by and cause me to long for his familiar smell.

Mom must have felt bored one day when she decided it was a good idea to teach me how to draw. The first few times she stuck a charcoal pencil in my mouth, I thought she meant for me to have a good chew. Naturally, the idea of drawing pictures on a large sheet of paper hadn't occurred to me as a dignified occupation for a herding dog. We went through several pencils before I got the hang of running the thing across a piece of paper and then listen to Mom praise me like I was her moronic child learning to write the alphabet. I found it nearly impossible to curtail my high octane energy through a pencil. Nope. The open fields gave me happiness and allowed me to run at top speed feeling the breeze against my face and the wings on my feet, and now here I stood in a brightly lit room with a pencil stuck in my mouth being asked to draw a flower.

Unfortunately, HH made an unexpected visit to her studio and began laughing, which needless to say completed my humiliation. I could feel Mom's body go tense and knew she wasn't happy with his presence, so I got busy acting like drawing little flowers came natural to me and after a few appeared on the paper, Mom went ecstatic and HH leaned over in utter amazement.

"Wow, Heddy, you're a born teacher. And who could have thought Lambert would have the makings of a Monet."

"I knew it. Lambert can do anything. He's just brilliant, Daniel." She clapped her hands and they hugged while I drew a few more posies to keep the mood light. This artist shit really bored my hairy butt and left me exhausted from the anxiety of capturing the image in my mind and then rerouting it to something worth looking at. I hoped Mom didn't get out the colored pencils. Two hours later, sure enough, she hauled out the colored pencil set, and we spent the entire afternoon engrossed in my learning curve while HH trundled off to make a large pot of split pea soup, which would cause me to fart green for the next three days.

When the snow began to melt, Mom's spirits soared and we found ourselves outside roaming the countryside for interesting subjects to paint. Finally, I got some relief from my duties as a model before my butt became permanently numb from inactivity and the hardwood floor. I loved scouting the countryside, especially when we stopped and Mom watched while I ran through someone else's fields and jumped over their fences, not my most graceful move being built so low to the ground but I enjoyed it. Suddenly, the memories came rushing back to me when I saw a small herd of sheep and a pretty black and white dog herding them toward a barn.

I ran to Mom and jumped in the car. I couldn't control my tears and one or two dropped on the seat where Mom, being highly observant, noticed the small droplets of water containing a lifetime of sadness. She sat beside me and stroked my body, but I sank further into despair over all the times my heroic, older brother licked the top of my head with his arms wrapped around my body; he smelled of warmth and the sweet breath of a puppy. Now that his scent lay fresh in my mind, I knew it was time to hit the road with my dog backpack and water bottle. I turned and gave Mom's face a thorough licking to last until I returned. We drove home silently, and I waited until the moon lit the bedroom walls before packing for my journey, but first I stopped in Mom's studio and tried to leave her a message so she wouldn't worry. I picked up one of the charcoal pencils and drew a primitive picture of a small dog. I didn't want her to think I had wandered outside by accident and became lost on my way back home. I wanted her to know I had a purpose and would be back soon. Although, time slipped away from me when fraught with a purpose bigger than the daily efforts I made to keep everyone in the same room while I stationed myself on alert nearby in case of an emergency. So far, all emergencies have been of the emotional variety and disappeared after a few histrionics and an intense barking fit, the latter expressed by Yours Truly.

I shoved some of HH's homemade bread and a chunk of raw cheese in my backpack along with my water bottle. Strapping the thing over my shoulders seemed to be beyond my patience so I let it hang around my neck and tried not to look stupid as I hit the road with my nose in the air sniffing out the most traffic on 95. I had mixed feelings about being at large in the world. Mostly, I felt the humming of fear when hearing the night traffic and smelling the gasoline coming off the cars, which could easily veer off the road and plow into me, leaving my body looking as flat as road kill. I remembered Harry telling me repeatedly to stay away from people and follow along the road but not on it. Easier said than done when discovering I had to make my way through the underbrush and avoid falling into small ponds.

After several hours of being on the move, I got a whiff of the pretty dog I had seen earlier herding her sheep. I spotted her standing on a grassy knoll that looked perfect for a picnic. She eyed me curiously while I reached into my bag and dragged out the hunk of cheese and nosed it in her direction. She sniffed it, probably to make sure it didn't have mold growing on it, and then I remembered she was an actual working dog and wouldn't have the refined tastes of Yours Truly and was probably sniffing for poison. To put her mind at ease, I bit off a chunk first and laid down beside her to have a go at it. I tried to act casual but my mind kept going to her smell, creating an odd sensation in my undercarriage. The next thing I knew we were rolling around on the ground with her trying to show me exactly what I was supposed to be doing with my animal zoo. Previous to this encounter, I had only humped the vacuum cleaner and a few fence posts, which left me with an empty feeling and the slight sense I had just made a fool of myself. Finally, when exhaustion overtook us and the sheep began to act spooked by our contretemps, we shoved up together on the ground; I now knew what it felt like to be married and in love.

I told her all about my heroic, older brother and my determination to find him. I even told her about Mom, HH, and the two fur balls who lived in the same house with me and by the time I had finished expressing my own importance in the family unit, you'd have thought that I was the one who paid the mortgage. She said I had an easy life and that she would love to live where she could decide what she wanted to do every morning instead of being told by her owner, who she said, possessed a strong notion about a dog's place being in the field next to the sheep. We both glanced over at her herd. They now appeared to be indifferent to our presence and were grinding away on the grass peeking through a light layer of snow on the ground.

I could have spent the entire day doing nothing with my new wife but we both had a purpose; I promised her I would be back in a short while after first asking her name. She said her owner called her Daisy but she preferred to be called Pretty by anyone who cared enough to ask, so I called her Pretty. I pressed my nose to her body and sniffed the scent from her fur hoping it would get me through the hard days to come. My head dithered in the clouds of love for the first few miles and then began to settle my feet to the ground when encountering a nasty bramble bush.

I left my hanky for Pretty to sniff so she wouldn't forget me. I knew I would never lose the scent of a dog that showed me a different kind of affection than my older brother had but somehow just as poignant. One day ran into the other while I hid in sheds and drank from creek beds. My stomach growled for food but nothing grew on the tail end of winter, so the only thing left to do was forage from the kitchen farm houses. I got shot at twice for sticking my face in a cherry pie and grabbing a loaf of bread from a stranger's table but it kept me going. I hardly had a spare moment to think about my position on the NRA, especially when noticing the hunters were also at large and created another source of danger for me.

I heard the jack rabbits running for cover and the birds screeching about all the carnivores let loose in the woods carrying guns. Eventually, I realized the dog grapevine extended to the birds in the trees watching for any idiot with a gun. I tuned in and asked for safety tips from the same said birds that were a nuisance to the farmers when eating their seeds. I, too, began to take a higher vantage point of my surroundings; mostly I appreciated the loveliness of nature and during these musings would nearly come up short of a shotgun if I had not been forewarned by the safety committee sitting in the treetops. I stopped this bucolic dithering after a few close calls and really got down to the business of survival. I knew if I ever made it back to Mom again, I would never leave. Even the fur balls and Thomas Jefferson occupied a soft spot in my heart. I soldiered on.

More days passed with me wandering through the woods sniffing every smell that wafted by my nose and even sticking my nose in places where it didn't belong. I had an unfortunate experience with a squirrel in the knot hole of a large tree. Afterwards, I laid low for several days until the teeth marks healed along with the beating my nerves had taken by the aggressive squirrel, but I supposed from his point of view I did appear dangerous. Most of the time, I kept the smell of 95 in the background so I would know I hadn't gone too far off course, but one day I found myself so far up a dirt road I thought I had reached Canada and then suddenly a familiar smell came my way. I continued toward the smell until spotting the shiny truck I had seen at the urban barnyards.

I decided to pay attention to my primal instincts for a change and circle the perimeter before running head long into unfamiliar territory. The squirrel had been a good teacher if I were inclined to take a Zen approach to my wounded nose. I now knew a wise dog remained present to all dangers. I ran along the fence line and while the bleating of sheep was familiar and their dusty, muggy smell hadn't changed, this was definitely not the haphazard operation Idiot Farmer ran. The sheep had been divided up into several pastures, each with its own supply of creek water running through the individual pasture lands and had been damned up in some places to slow the water down. The fences, in contrast to Idiot Farmer's barbed wire nightmares, were white railing that looked like something surrounding the Kentucky race horse pasture land.

I ran along the other side until coming upon the smell of my heroic, older brother. I moved my eyes along the horizon of sheep until I spotted him standing on the far side of his herd. I crawled under the fence and made my way around the butt end of the herd about forty yards away from my brother. I watched him work the sheep into a nice, neat crowd, all babies accounted for, and then he stood back and put his nose up in the air. I knew he caught a whiff of me; all the beauty products had long faded leaving nothing but my natural odor. His head jerked sideways and suddenly he flew toward me, feet not touching the ground, a blur of black and white energy full of love and familiarity coming in my direction. I sprinted toward him, hesitant at first, noticing his size being much larger than when we were puppies. We both stopped abruptly and stared at each other, and then he brought a paw up over my neck and pulled me toward him. I must have looked like a whiny baby when beginning to shed tears of relief. He licked my face with such affection, more tears fell, and I just collapsed on the ground where he stayed beside me for the rest of the day while keeping one eye on his herd grazing nearby.

15

"DANIEL!" I could hear myself shriek after searching for Lambert to go for his morning walk. Daniel came running to find me clutching Lambert's stuffed toy. I remembered the cute way he had picked out the stuffed animal during our first visit to Karma's store. "Lambert's missing. He's not here. He's not outside or anywhere! He's been stolen. I just know it!"

"Have you looked in every room, sweetie?" I watched Daniel glance at his cats as though they could shed some light on Lambert's disappearance. They remained unconcerned on the couch in their usual spots. In fact, they didn't bother opening their eyes to acknowledge Daniel's calling to them and asking if they had seen their new brother since last night. Nothing. They remained mute, except for a small interior fuss over the reference to Lambert being their brother. I knew they both probably felt revolted over the possibility that a freak of nature had occurred in their lineage.

"No, honey, I was so upset that I forgot the studio." We ran to the studio but could not find Lambert in any of his usual spots. I began to cry against my new husband's chest; I cried quietly at first, and then I could hear my cries turn into sobs.

Daniel held me tight while studying the room for clues. When his eyes fell upon the primitive drawing of a dog on the floor next to the French doors, he said. "Sweetie, look." He left me to dry my tears on my pajama sleeve and picked up the drawing. It had a charcoal paw smudge in the corner. "Is this one of yours?" he asked. We stood squinting at the odd looking dog with a few dark spots drawn on it.

"No! Maybe it's from Lambert. He's left us a message!" I responded. My voice must have gone up two octaves in my excitement.

"It's definitely a picture of a Border Collie. Look at the dark spots." We continued looking at Lambert's dog doodle in an effort to understand its meaning. "Either this is a self-portrait or he's gone in search of this dog."

I ran from the room and returned seconds later yelling to Daniel, "His backpack and water bottle are missing. He planned this. Sure as anything. My baby boy left me. I just can't bear it." I dropped to the floor and sobbed with such anguish, tears came to Daniel's eyes as he bent to console me. I could feel his tears drop onto the back of my pajama top despite the hysteria I felt at having been abandoned my dog.

We stayed in this position for a few minutes and then finally Daniel spoke. "It's best to take immediate action." He was right, of course, the situation called for a lot of action. I tore from the studio and went straight to the phone.

"Yes, let's call the police. They can put out an amber alert!" I shouted at my new husband who ran along on my heels to stand next to me while I dialed 911.

"Oh, sweetie, they only do that for children. We'll start by calling the local shelters and ask all of Lambert's friends to help with the search." He took the phone and called the police business number and requested a list of local shelters and their numbers.

Two hours later, the house was full of concerned friends making calls and gathering flyers to post. Jack whimpered on the couch with Isabel and Philomena, who were mildly irritated at his presence, but I could tell they also felt sorry for the odd looking, little dog. A thought occurred to me when glancing over at the couch, and I spoke with some meaning but also feeling slightly ridiculous at having verbalized the thought, "Too bad Jack can't talk. Lambert probably told him where he was going."

"Oh, but Jack can talk. He talks all the time to his animal communicator," Sally said. "Why don't we call and have her come here and ask him questions?" We all stared at Sally, except Karma. She had just hung up the phone from her conversation with Guard Dogs for Hire, inquiring as to whether or not they had any sniffers to rent. She announced they did and would have two here at the given address within the hour. I felt a sense of relief something concrete was being done by professionals, who probably wouldn't be floundering around like a bunch of amateur detectives going about an investigative task in a willy-nilly fashion. I could feel a heaviness descend on my chest. It hampered my breathing. My breaths became rapid and shallow.

"It's true, Heddy," Karma said. "Communicators are used mostly by horse breeders to help diagnose physical symptoms. It can narrow down the problem area and allow vets to treat them without the expense of an MRI. And, too, people use them for lost animals and neurotic pets. A really good one is invaluable."

Daniel and I looked at the two women like they had lost their minds but Mr. Dodder saved the day by tossing in his two cents worth. "Yuh gotta do everthin, Heddy, tuh git yuh dog back. Wuth a try." His words calmed me, and I began to feel the heaviness lift.

Sally called Jack's communicator, Karma picked out one of Lambert's most endearing photos and designed a poster on her laptop, and Daniel and I followed the two dog sniffers all over the fields. Even Mr. Dodder threw himself to the task of locating Lambert. He called what he referred to as his mobile geezer friends and had them out scouring the country side looking for a lost Border Collie carrying a backpack.

The sniffer dogs put their noses to the ground and followed after their utility snouts with the intensity of a SWAT team without weapons and with considerably more fervor in applying their natural gifts of being able to smell a gnat within a five mile radius. Daniel and I ran along behind them carrying Lambert's bedding in case they needed their olfactory memory revived. They didn't, which was made obvious when both dogs began digging in the far corner of the field. They dug down three feet forcing the handler and us to stand back from the onslaught of wet dirt flying out of the ground. The sniffers dug furiously until recovering four small, black leather shoes with tiny buckles covered in teeth marks. The handler held them in front of me, and then all I saw was myself collapsing to the ground, unconscious and in need of a doctor. Fortunately, Daniel had spent the morning with his cell phone stuck in his ear and quickly dialed his EMT friend two farms down the road. He carried me back to the house and laid my nearly lifeless body on the couch. When I woke up later, I remember asking if I had fallen gracefully, which was a strange question coming from me because I didn't usually worry about how I'm being perceived by others and, in fact, prefer to remain oblivious to their perspective when it comes to my appearance, as mentioned earlier. Altogether, I thought my behavior over the disappearance of Lambert a normal response to a missing loved one. Of course, I would have preferred to be anesthetized during the entire period of our separation.

Later, Sally told me that when Jack saw Lambert's wedding shoes, he began to whimper and turn in circles on the rug. Eventually, she said, he got himself into such a high state of anxiety that he, too, collapsed on the floor next to me lying on the couch.

She also said Daniel seemed slightly hysterical himself when seeing her lean over her unconscious dog checking to see if he needed mouth to mouth. "Please, hurry the communicator. Maybe she can get to the bottom of all this emotion over Lambert's shoes." Just then Daniel's EMT neighbor arrived at the front door, letting himself inside to find our two unconscious bodies in need of ministering. I could feel him pick up my wrist in search of a pulse, although I wouldn't have cared if he had revived Jack first.

"Pulse is normal. Did she have a shock?" The big burly man asked. I could hear his gruff voice through my fog and feel his warm breath on my face.

Then I heard the sweet sounds of my new husband, an instant later to be interrupted by the gruff voice. "Yes, too complicated to explain in a few words,"

"And the little dog on the floor? Same shock?" Suddenly I smelled a sharp, obnoxious odor that woke me up with a start and for a second I didn't know where I was and became even more confused when looking down and seeing a large burly man holding a tiny bottle under Jack's nose.

Jack and I sat up and looked at each other. I held out my arms to him; he jumped on my lap and placed his head against my stomach and began whimpering while I petted his little head. Everyone stood staring at us with concerned faces, especially strained around the eyes. I knew they had been working hard to find Lambert and that, they too, felt the unease of a dog gone missing. My baby boy made my heart cry just to think about that sweet face always looking up at me in the morning times as we trotted along going hither and yon enjoying each other's company. I began to cry again. Daniel sat beside me and put his arm around my shoulders. Jack cried louder. I could barely hear Daniel talking to me over mine and Jack's rhapsodic whimpering.

"Heddy, you're going to have to be strong and try to understand whatever drove Lambert to pack his bag is important enough to leave you and will probably only take a short time before he's finished his business and will be back home with us." Daniel usually doesn't put so many words in one sentence, and he's rarely been emphatic about anything except his desire to have a family of any animal and people combination. This thought brought my attention straight back to Lambert. I didn't even know Lambert had business besides being my constant companion but nothing that required him to step outside the family confines. The more I thought about my dog's behavior, it made me realize again how little I knew about him. Perhaps, I should have become friends with the old farmer and made an effort to be privy to Lambert's past. Just like white families who adopt babies from different cultures but keep their cultures alive by hanging posters of their indigenous beginnings artistically displayed throughout their suburban houses. Daniel had even suggested getting sheep. Maybe a small herd of sheep would have kept Lambert happy and at home, but then I remembered Lambert was happy and when we were at the barnyards, he seemed only interested in the truck that drove away with a dog sitting in the front seat. I remembered the dog looked at Lambert briefly from the back window before the truck disappeared amid the traffic.

"Oh honey, it must be the dog in the truck that Lambert chased? The one that man had said looked like Lambert. It must have been one of his relatives. The dog, I mean." I was so excited.

"Yes, I remember, sweetie. Lambert was sure intent on catching up. You're right. Can you recall where you found Lambert tied to the vegetable stand?"

"No, just the general area, and besides it isn't growing season now. The old farmer wouldn't be there." My thoughts suffered just a glimmer of hope and then moved along to take in Lambert's drawing. Maybe that was his mother or another relative, the one in the truck, and he felt compelled to find him. I had no idea dogs became so attached to each other that their hearts would long to be with them, that their hearts would break from the love of a lost friend. I then realized I had taken Lambert for granted, treated him like I was enough for him and didn't give any thought to the nurturing of his private relationships. Then I looked down at Jack. "When's the animal communicator coming?" I glanced at Sally, who stood wringing her hands.

"Oh, dear Heddy. She can't come until tomorrow. She's in conference with the local canine unit. Apparently, they've not been performing up to snuff due to morale issues." My face must have fallen over hearing this news.

"Sweetie, let's use the time to go in search of the old farmer at the vegetable stand. Meanwhile, maybe our friends wouldn't mind putting up some flyers. There are no Border Collies in the shelters right now. They said they would call us if one came in." Sally picked up Jack, and Daniel reached for my hand and led me toward the bedroom to shower and dress. I could hear everyone's voices calling after us not to worry that they would keep working on 'Project Lambert'.

Daniel and I drove along the country roads in hopes I could spot something that looked familiar. The sniffers followed along in a truck behind us with an open communication device put in place so we could hear them bark if their noses caught a familiar smell. So far, nothing. Then suddenly I saw an old hand-written sign with Vegetables for Sale nailed to a tree. Daniel pulled the car off the road and we got out to take a look joined by the sniffers whose noses worked overtime running along the ground and coming to a complete halt at exactly the same location where Lambert had sat waiting for someone to want him. I studied the ground and noticed the imprint of table legs the size of the banquet table the old farmer had used to hold his vegetables. The dogs began barking and for a second, I felt the spirit of hope, a jubilant feeling of anticipation that Lambert and I would be reunited in a short time.

"See, look," I said and pointed toward the ground. "This is where Lambert was sitting. You can tell by the dent in the soil where the table had been placed. " Daniel hugged me and the dogs continued to bark ecstatically and I wondered for a second if they knew why they were barking but after living with Lambert for eight months, I believed dogs understood more than we did, much to my own chagrin and delight. Emotions descended on me during the few seconds we stood in the place where I had met Lambert for the first time; the two men moved closer together and discussed what to do next.

"Let's check the neighboring farms and ask if one of them had sold vegetables in this area and also we can show them Lambert's picture," Daniel said.

The first farm sent the sniffers into a frenzy of barking and so Daniel ran back to their truck to ask the handler to keep them in the cab until we scoped out the place. It appeared in need of repair, poor even, with tractor tires laying on the front yard and a paddock filled with unhappy sheep guarded by a vigilant Border Collie. That could have been Lambert's life I thought, allowing my mind to run through all sorts of scenarios of how Lambert's life might have played out if I hadn't come along and took him for my companion. I had no idea that's what he would become. The more my thoughts traveled over this idea, the more I realized Lambert had shaped our relationship into something comfortable for both of us. I convinced myself he didn't miss herding sheep and that he really was on an important mission that would eventually be made known to those of us who loved him.

A raggedy woman answered the door and looked at us like we had come from a government office intending to put a bypass through her land. I tried to smile at the worn out face but the distrustful expression had turned sour and was so off-putting, that I just shut down altogether and let Daniel do the talking. He immediately showed the old woman the picture of Lambert.

"Does this dog look familiar at all? My wife purchased him from a farmer selling vegetables over on Half Mile Road last summer. He's disappeared and we thought he might want to come back to his first home." Daniel sounded sweet and displayed such a gentle, non-threatening manner that couldn't possibly upset the old woman.

"He wouldn't want to come back here. Useless as the day is long." She slammed the door in our faces, which gave us both a shock but at least we knew this was Lambert's humble beginnings. Now, I understood why Lambert acted like he had died and gone to heaven the first time he had set foot in my car and made himself comfortable in the front passenger seat. Just then a grizzled old man came sauntering around the barn.

"What's the commotion?" he shouted at us. "Can hear them dogs in the back pasture. Shut 'em up." Immediately the handler gave them some kind of command that indicated their job was done for now, which resulted in silence.

Daniel went through the same routine with the husband as he had done with his wife, using a kind, soft spoken manner. However, the result was the same.

"Runt of the litter, that one. No use looking here. Wouldn't have him back if he were of a mind to come." He didn't so much as talk as he did bark, putting emphatic punctuation marks after each phrase. I could see up his nostrils; they looked stained from tobacco with rust-colored nose hairs that probably never had a chance to turn as white as his stringy hair.

"What happened to his brothers and sisters?" I piped up finally getting ahold of a few words.

"Sold 'em all to sheep farmers from here to the Dakotas." He moved toward the house.

"Could we have their information, Mister? We just want to find our dog," I said in a pleading voice.

"Nope. People like their privacy. Best move along." He disappeared into his house. Daniel and I walked back to the car. We spent the rest of the day following the sniffers around the countryside in hopes of picking up another more recent scent of Lambert's whereabouts. Eventually, we gave up for the day and drove back home.

The next morning, everyone gathered in the living room for their assignments, but first we waited in a flutter of excitement in anticipation of the visit from Jack's communicator. Sally greeted her at the door along with Jack, whose nerves still seemed jangled from the anxiety caused by his missing friend. She appeared like a normal, well-dressed woman in her forties, not that I expected her to be bohemian or wearing a peasant dress with a scooped neck cotton blouse, although, when studying her shoes, I noticed she was wearing what retailers now call Vegan Footwear intended to supply animal lovers with shoes that have a guilt free spin to their stylish shoes similar to the hemp wedgies of the 1970s. She sat across from Jack, who had ensconced himself between Isabel and Philomena. I had no idea why Jack took comfort from the two cats. They barely opened their eyes but I did notice Philomena put her paw gently on Jack's own paw, and I swear she patted him like a mother consoling her baby. This just proved I knew nothing about an animal's interior life but was about to find out the minute Jack's communicator opened her mouth to speak his words.

"He's gone. He's gone. I helped him bury his shoes. They hurt his paws and embarrassed him."

"Can you ask him if he knows where Lambert has gone?" I said. The communicator turned to Jack and barely got out the first two words before Jack flew back with a hysterical response, began whimpering and then gave up all together and shoved his face against Philomena searching for comfort.

"He says Lambert loved his heroic, older brother. Said his brother saved him from drowning. Says Lambert misses his older brother. He wants him to live with his Mom and HH." The communicator kept translating Jack's answers without faltering.

"Whose HH?" I asked.

"The man who eats only vegetables and loves his Mom. Jack says HH is good to Lambert and good to Lambert's Mom. He is saying something about an old codger."

I cut off Jack's rambling right there before he said something regrettable about Sally's new friend. "Where's Lambert? Is he with his brother?" I asked Jack directly but heard nothing and so the animal communicator relayed Jack's message.

"Lambert's in the woods. He's happy but he misses his Mom." The communicator finished this last sentence seconds before Jack collapsed and passed out again. Everyone stared at him in disbelief, and then finally I remembered Johns had given me several of Charo's pills for my nerves; I ran and got one to shove down Jack's lifeless gullet. Poor little guy, I thought, and shook my head sympathetically and took one of Charo's pills to calm my own nerves.

The communicator told us Jack's nerves couldn't take much more and that he wanted an animal healer like Thomas Jefferson and something about getting on the dog grapevine tonight when he felt better. He also said he and Lambert are afraid of Maggie the Butcher. She looked puzzled but Sally and I knew exactly what he meant. Jack's colonoscopy came to mind along with Lambert running from a tranquilizer gun. I realized sorrowfully that I had made some mistakes and assumptions when caring for my beloved companion. I loved the idea of Lambert telling me what he thought like I could understand him as well as the communicator, who now stood looking down at Jack with an appreciative expression on her pretty face. She thanked him and asked the angels to bless him. Yesterday, I might have laughed and dismissed the idea of angelic beings surrounding us with love, but today I thought about asking a few of Jack's angels to lift my own forlorn spirit.

The communicator left us in silence until finally Mr. Dodder spoke, "Wuh need to get busy putting up flyers.

Nuvuh gunna find him suttin on the couch, Heddy." Daniel agreed and went to the phone to call the newspapers and ask them if they would run a full page ad offering a $5000 reward for a missing Border Collie who answers to the name of Lambert. I nearly cried over this loving gesture but my own phone rang with Johns calling from his busy salon to ask if Jack was helpful. I thought the little guy was helpful in many ways but it was clear he didn't know Lambert's exact location and at that moment, I realized our vet had been remiss in not putting a tracking device on Lambert, especially with all that fuss made over his ability to impregnate every lusty female from here to Canada. We would address both issues upon Lambert's return, not to mention, the need to search for a more compatible vet.

The days began to follow the same routine for weeks. Sally made a bed up near Thomas Jefferson for Jack and had him talk to the animal communicator during the times his nerves quieted down long enough to answer questions but his answers still sounded nonsensical bordering on moments of hysteria at any suggestion his friend may not return; Mr. Dodder and his mobile unit traveled the country side looking for Lambert; Johns showed Lambert's photo to all of his clients, until finally taping it to his mirror for all his clients to see the second they sat down in his chair; Karma passed out the flyers to all of her customers; Daniel learned how to care for sheep so Lambert would have a small herd waiting for him upon his return; and I woke up every morning in a fit of tears and then began my day walking along all the paths Lambert and I had enjoyed during happier times together and when I finished walking, I threw myself into making phone calls to shelters, newspapers, and outlying police departments until finally reaching the Dakotas. A grumpy-sounding sheriff laughed at me when I asked if I could send him a photo of Lambert to pass on to his deputies and the state police. He said they had more to do out there than search for somebody's pampered pet. I probably shouldn't have mentioned Lambert's backpack and travel bottle having long since run out of water. Other states had been more accommodating by hanging Lambert's photograph in the local post office. I wasn't sure how I felt about the implication of him placed on the FBI's Most Wanted but any public display of a sadly missed family member was better than nothing. After spending the morning making phone calls, I addressed the hundreds of emails from sympathetic dog owners, the state police, and a few mercenary con artists regarding Lambert's whereabouts unknown.

When Daniel and I finished our long days, we sat huddled up together on the couch near the two unconcerned napping cats. Finally, my mental light bulb had shown brighter than it had in sometime when I came upon the idea of asking the communicator to talk to Philomena and Isabel. Daniel called her, somewhat skeptical, but willing to try anything and the dear woman was at the house in thirty minutes whispering in their listless ears.

"They're both talking at once saying he's with his older brother and some bimbo he met at a sheep farm. They said he and his brother are on their way home. And something about not wanting to live with a pack of dogs and life not being the same since Lambert's arrival but that he is a good dog but he hovers too much. They also say he talks to them every day on the dog grapevine, passing along information they are supposed to give to his Mom." I asked her about the dog grapevine and she mentioned it was telepathic communication among animals. I pondered this thought for a second while Philomena and Isabel caught a breath before ending their diatribe on the inconvenience of having their naps interrupted by a stranger and could she come back later when they were both well-rested. I wondered well-rested from what, but my excitement over the possibility everything they said was true made me love them despite their irascible dispositions. I sighed with relief in Daniel's arms after thanking the communicator and asking her to stay for supper. She said she was on her way to talk a therapy dog off a ledge. "The poor thing feels unloved and says he's tired of being someone else's eyeballs, especially a grumpy old man who does nothing but complain about missing the good old days and all the women who inhabited them." She went on to tell us often times a therapy dog's life consisted of nothing but a series of automaton tasks that bored the smartest and most loving dogs. She said something about animals having souls same as people and then instructed us to wait a few days, and she would have another chat with our cats and then she closed the front door behind her.

Daniel and I threw our arms around each other and wept with joy. We each grabbed a cat and kissed the disinterested face staring back at us and then we threw ourselves back on the couch to imagine the reunion of Lambert with his older brother. I could hear myself sigh with contentment and total faith in Lambert finding his way home.

16

Lambert Weighs In:

All I ever heard the fancy farmer call my heroic, older brother was Buddy. "Come on, Buddy. Good boy, Buddy. Thatta boy, Buddy. Back to the barn, Buddy." Of course, I heard all these short he-man sentences while hiding behind the nearest bush wherever my brother happened to be herding his sheep. I told him I didn't think Buddy a proper Highland name for a dog of his breeding, but he just shrugged and said he didn't have my polish and refined manner. I hadn't thought of myself in this light and I have to confess I puffed up some when hearing myself being described similar to an English butler. Shortly after my bout of self-importance, one of Buddy's sheep came up behind me and kicked my refined butt into the nearest watering hole. My coat already looked like it had been left in the woods for the winter, so this little contretemps just added a few more knots to my rat's nest. I could actually hear myself being described as something the cat dragged in. Isabel and Philomena would have a field day of sarcasm when seeing me, and poor Johns would put his face in his hands and weep from knowing he would have to take his electric clippers to trim my 'lovely hair' right down to my pink skin.

I checked in with the two fur balls often on the dog grapevine. Their ability to receive information astounded me at first, and then I began to feel some comfort in knowing they would pick up the phone whenever I called. Not so with my good friend Jack. I could only hear static and a great deal of whimpering when I tried reaching him. The fur balls told me he had been spending his days with Thomas Jefferson, because he felt abandoned by his only friend. I shed a few tears upon hearing about Jack's anguish. He was always a sensitive little guy. I still kept trying to get ahold of him though, so I could reassure him I was returning soon. Actually, I had lost my bearings and sense of time. Not only that, Buddy hadn't decided whether or not to come and live with me and Mom. I didn't bother to mention the extended family for fear of alarming him. After all, he had spent his entire adult life taking care of sheep and sleeping under the stars. It wasn't my idea of a life well-lived but felt sure HH would make adequate accommodations for Buddy's sleeping arrangements. He would probably screen in the back porch and add a couple of sky lights for Buddy to look up at the stars. I may love my brother, but nothing appealed to me more right now than snuggling next to Mom and spending the night in her warmth.

I decided to have another brotherly talk with Buddy. After all, I had to think about making my way home soon. The moment the sheep were down for the night, I began describing his new idyllic life. I even threw in some people stuff about where do you see yourself in five years? He looked at me like I had a screw loose and then began laughing. Of course, I realized I sounded desperate, pathetic even, like a striving over-achiever, looking for the security package and buying extended care insurance. Even I knew the Big Guy had a hand in everything including the future I wanted my heroic, older brother to be part of. Finally, Buddy relented and said he needed a couple of days to consider what to do with the sheep. He even asked for my help in transferring them to a field closer to the main barn. I thought this sounded grueling but decided it would definitely be worth the effort and not only that, it would give me an opportunity to strut my sheep dog stuff. After all, it may not be my preference but somewhere past the country airs resided my real barnyard self.

Buddy and I only walked a few miles on our first day before I had to rest my tired butt. I may have made a mistake in romanticizing my brief foray into sheep herding; Buddy had to spend most of his time rescuing me from somebody's touchy mother. How was I supposed to know sheep mothers practiced attachment parenting? I just thought the baby sheep would be easier to herd because of their small size.

Fortunately, before leaving the fancy farmer, Buddy had grabbed a bag of cookies and a block of cheese from the bunk house to put in my backpack. I lay panting under the noon sun, nibbling on some cheese while my heroic, older brother worked at catching the smell off my backpack to help find our way home. Once in a while, he would check in with Harry at Missing Persons to get an idea of latitude and longitude. I had no clue how the two of them figured out all this stuff, and so naturally felt some relief in not having to tax my mental capacity. At this point, I knew I was running on empty. Then I remembered Pretty.

I sent her some messages over the dog grapevine to let her know I was on my way, but she must have been too busy to tune in and listen to me nattering on like a love sick puppy. I had heard Johns use that phrase when discovering Charo had a boyfriend. A love sick puppy was just what I felt like but didn't mention it to Buddy for fear of sounding girly. I didn't want him to have second thoughts about following me home to a place the complete opposite of his rustic abode. I worried about there being enough to keep him busy. His work ethic put HH to shame and left me panting after a couple of hours galloping over the hills and dales. He seemed to have a better sense of direction than I did and his ability to travel toward my own scent while having me at his side would astound the navigation experts.

We slept at night after first swapping stories. I loved hearing about his sheep herding adventures but noticed he never seemed to be attached to any of his charges and spent most of his time working and very little time indulging in self-reflection. I wondered if he had been lonely for someone to reach down and stroke the side of his face or give him a good butt scratch. HH knew I liked him to scratch the top of my butt near the tail. It never seemed to bother him that he was actually scratching a dog's butt or even when we walked in town and he would be carrying my poop around in a small biodegradable bag until reaching the nearest trash can. Sometimes HH would stick my bag of poop in his coat pocket and forget about it until he put his coat on again to go someplace. He just laughed when he discovered my droppings nestled in his pocket and then he would toss them on the mulch pile like they possessed value. You got to love a human person who carried a dog's poop. People from other cultures might think our people had gotten confused over hierarchy. After all, if the tables were turned, I'm not sure I would want to carry HH's royal droppings in a little plastic bag. I knew

Buddy had only used the woods for his toilet so was in for a real treat when seeing the Lord of the Manor picking up after him. I smiled at the thought.

I noticed Buddy always slept close to me and sometimes would lay a paw over my back and even press his face against mine before going to sleep. I loved him for remembering I was his brother, and I loved him for always trying to make me feel wanted by him. I had to curtail the sloppy sentimentality in our conversations for fear of his discovering I was a needy dog with the heart of a romantic. Buddy even worked to get the knots out of my fur by clamping his teeth firmly on them and pulling. Hurt like hell, but I noticed the area he kept working on was looking better and sure eased the pain.

Finally, the day came when I got a whiff of Pretty. Her sweet, lady dog smell made my head feel light and my grubby paws lift off the ground in a bout of love so strong Buddy stopped and stared at me like I was about to levitate to regions unknown. He bumped up against my side, but I wouldn't be deterred from running in the direction of Pretty's familiar scent, prompting Buddy to take off after me, and suddenly we both stopped short when seeing her laying outside a small barn on a pile of hay with two tiny puppies romping over her body. When she took in my familiar smell, her head turned sideways and her tail began to wag at the sight of me. My heart leaped from happiness at seeing my Pretty and our babies using their mother as a launching pad to jump in the hay. I lowered my body to the ground and moved toward her slunk so close to the grass I looked like I had done something wrong, but unless one of our offspring was simple-minded, I also felt a moment of pride when knowing I was now head of my own progeny. I began kissing Pretty and cleaning up her coat, wanting to make myself useful and also wanting her to feel like I wasn't something she had imagined passing through her life and leaving her a single mother of two. Nope. I decided right then and there to take Pretty and our babies home with me.

I turned to tell Buddy but he was busy playing with his niece and nephew, who made me smile inside at our new Border Collie family. Eventually, we had the family pow-wow and everyone came to the same agreement about proceeding to the farmette and settling there along with Mom and HH. Again, I neglected to mention the fur balls, Jack, and Thomas Jefferson, and the old codger seemed too much to describe, so I didn't bother figuring him into the extended family equation. Buddy asked for a couple of days to check out the food situation, leaving me well hid in the small barn. He thought it best to fill our stomachs in the meantime, which required him to sneak inside the family residence while they worked in the fields and raid the pantry. We feasted on crusty, homemade bread, a box of cereal, and half a coconut possessing a nice flavor but didn't seem worth the effort when having to dig out the meat clinging to the sides of a hairy shell. I worked at scrubbing off the outer debris of a few pieces to give to Pretty. She smiled sweetly at me causing me to feel another stirring of passion, which I immediately dashed with a few seconds of reason and some consideration for the mother of my new progeny.

Buddy managed to fill my backpack with enough food to get us home. Since I had first seen Pretty when riding along the countryside with Mom while scouting for idyllic painting subjects, I knew we couldn't be too far from home. My heart leapt at the thought of being with Mom again and hearing her soft voice tell me how much she missed me and, too, I just could hardly wait for her to meet the rest of my dog family. I had no doubt they would be welcomed and even pampered with HH's vegetarian chili soup. We began to travel.

Buddy and I picked up a puppy and carried them along in our mouths. They squirmed like anything, so we rearranged the food supply and shoved them into my backpack, which had slipped from all the weight to hang heavily around my neck, nearly dragging along the ground. This slowed us down some, but Pretty needed to move at an amble and feed our progeny whenever they became restless. Poor Buddy. He nearly jumped from his skin at having to rein in his normal go-to speed, but he understood the necessity and slowed his pace.

Several days later, we could see the farmette. We stayed at a distance to study the lay of the land at which time I noticed several unfamiliar objects shaped like sheep grazing in the front pasture. They appeared unusually clean for sheep, which prior to seeing this beauty salon lot, I had only been around dusty brown wool balls, so the difference left me a little leery about what was waiting for us. Then I saw HH come outside and approach the gate but the second he swung it open, the small herd bolted to the other end of the field and dove straight through his neat and tidy split rail fence. HH went hollering after them, but they appeared hell bent on going to the next county, and then I saw Mom come outside and run faster than I had ever seen her run. She caught up to HH and together they chased after the frightened sheep.

Their clumsy herding efforts saddened my heart and made me look like a real maverick when it came to rounding up pretty much anything with legs. While I was busy aggrandizing my herding ability, suddenly, Buddy sprang into action and jumped the fence to head off the sheep before they went through the neighbor's fence and risked being blind-sided by their Black Angus bull. Buddy executed a neat turn and had them all scampering back toward the front pasture. My heroic, older brother defined poetry in motion. I whimpered from pride. I couldn't believe my good fortune in having my brother home with me. Pretty licked the side of my face, reminding me life just couldn't get any better.

I watched while Buddy helped HH secure the fence after corralling the sheep in the paddock. Mom petted Buddy and then looked up over our small hill to see me standing now with my progeny hung around my neck and my bride at my side. I hurried us toward Mom who was running to beat the band and then we all came together in a pile of tears, recriminations, and sloppy words of gratitude, mostly spoken by Mom who was a mess of emotion. HH and Buddy joined us. I gave Mom a few seconds to get use to the idea of two other dogs joining our pack before dumping my progeny at her feet. She squealed with delight and HH began laughing, and then he did the oddest thing by laying on the ground and letting the babies jump all over him, at which time Pretty licked one side of his face and Buddy licked the other, all done while I rested in Mom's arms, and after a few seconds, I felt the nudging of a flat face dog against my neck, and when I turned my head, I saw Jack. I tucked my head under Mom's arm and nearly wept from relief at knowing in my own small way, I had brought my entire family together and believed myself to be a herder of the longing heart.

The End

More books by the author:

A Chocolate Comedy

Solitary Pussytoes

Pretty Weeds

Women on Love

Coming soon:

<u>Novel</u>

The Wood Poet

Rooming House Blues

Made in the USA
Charleston, SC
24 November 2014